NIGHTMARE HALL

Sorority Sister

DIANE HOH

SCHOLASTIC INC.
New York Toronto London Auckland Sydney

ISBN 0-590-47689-0

12 11 10 9 8 7 6 5 4 3 2   4 5 6 7 8 9/9

Printed in the U.S.A.   01

First Scholastic printing, April 1994

NIGHTMARE HALL

Sorority Sister

Prologue

Omega Phi Delta.

Maxie ran her finger slowly over the letters on her new sorority sweatshirt.

She couldn't believe they'd actually pledged her. Out of all the girls who'd rushed Omega, she was one of the few — the lucky few — to be selected.

Everyone knew Omega Phi Delta was the best sorority on campus. Omegas were the coolest girls. They dated the most gorgeous guys and threw the wildest parties.

Becoming an Omega was like a dream come true for Maxie.

But the dream was about to become a nightmare.

Because something was terribly wrong at the Omega house.

Something deadly . . .

Chapter 1

It began slowly, with little things, so at first the sisters of Omega Phi Delta didn't even realize anything was wrong.

On Saturday morning, Maxie McKeon and Tinker Gabrielle were hanging out in their room at the Omega house, when Erica Bingham, Omega's president, appeared in the open doorway.

She was frowning. "I can't find my jewelry box," she informed the roommates. "Have either of you seen it? It's big, and lacquered in black with an Oriental print painted on the top, remember? Tinker, you said something about it when you were in my room last weekend."

"I said it was pretty," Tinker agreed. "You can't find it? How could you lose something that big?"

Erica stood up very straight, wide shoulders stiff in her gray university sweatshirt. "I didn't *lose* it, Tinker! It was on my dresser yesterday afternoon. I remember getting my pearl earrings out — the ones my grandmother gave me — to wear last night."

"Was the jewelry box there last night when you came home?" Maxie wanted to know. "When you took the earrings off?"

Erica shook her long, blonde pageboy. "I don't know. I was out dancing at Johnny's Place, and I was so tired when I got back, I just stuck the earrings on my dresser. I didn't notice the box was missing until I straightened my room this morning. I've been looking and looking, and I can't find it anywhere. Not only is it not on top of my dresser where it belongs, it is *not* in my room."

Maxie and Tinker exchanged a concerned glance. They were both thinking the same thing. Erica was the most organized person in the house. She was the one everyone else went to when they were hunting for a pair of scissors or the sewing kit or a flashlight. She always knew where everything was.

And now she couldn't find her own jewelry box?

"We'll help look," Maxie offered. In shorts, T-shirt, and bare feet, her dark hair bobbing on her shoulders, she padded down the hall with Erica and Tinker. "If we don't find it in fifteen minutes, you're on your own, Erica."

They didn't find the jewelry box.

Tears of frustration filled Erica's eyes. "The ring my grandmother gave me when I graduated from high school is in that box," she said.

"You didn't *lose* it, Erica," Maxie pointed out loyally. "You never lose anything. I think you should tell Mildred the box is missing."

Mildred was Mildred Booth, Omega Phi's housemother and cook. She would *not* be happy to hear that something of value was missing.

Maxie wasn't happy about it, either. She loved Omega house. Living in Lester dorm when she first arrived on the campus of Salem University had been fun. She'd made new friends there. But after the first Omega party, she knew this was where she belonged. The girls were all so nice and so much fun. She couldn't wait to belong. And once she'd been initiated she'd found it was ever better than she'd expected. She was proud to be seen in her Omega Phi sweatshirt. Now she always had a party to go to, a group to hang out with. College was more fun than ever.

It had been a major disappointment when Tinker hadn't been pledged at first. But halfway into the semester, one of the pledges had dropped out of school, and Tinker had gleefully taken her place, moving in with Maxie. Now, in March of second semester, Maxie could hardly remember living at Lester. If Jenna Dwyer, her ex-roommate at Lester and still her good friend, and Brendan Rafferty, her boyfriend, weren't around to remind her, she'd feel as if she'd always lived at Omega house.

And in all this time, from late October until the end of March, there had never been any trouble at the sorority house. None.

Now this. Erica's jewelry box missing. Maxie didn't like the way that made her feel. Off balance, as if the planet had suddenly tilted sideways. Or at least Omega house.

Maxie and Tinker went back to their room, telling Erica to come and get them if she needed support when she approached Mildred with the bad news.

"Keep looking and asking around in the meantime," Maxie suggested as they left Erica's room. "Maybe someone just borrowed it." But she didn't really think anyone would do that. Not without permission. A lot of borrowing went on in the house . . . clothes, hair dryers, class notes, occasionally even a few dollars, but never without asking first.

Their mood had changed when they returned to their room with the flowered wallpaper, white trim, and rose-colored carpet. A row of windows along the far wall let in ample sunlight on what had turned out to be a beautiful late-winter day.

"You don't think someone actually *took* Erica's jewelry box, do you?" Tinker asked nervously, running a hand through her very short, almost-white hair. A track athlete, Tinker, in direct contradiction to her name, was tall and broad-shouldered. Her real name was Belle. As a small child, her parents had nicknamed her Tinker Bell. When, as an adolescent, she experienced a sudden growth spurt, they refused to drop the nickname. Tinker seemed to find that really funny. "The Tinker Bell in Peter Pan is no bigger than my hand," she told Maxie laughingly. "When they say love is blind, they must mean parents."

"Do I think someone took the jewelry box?" Maxie asked. "I don't want to believe that someone took it. But we looked everywhere in that room. It's not that easy to lose something so large."

"We should ask around, see if anyone knows anything. Candie might know something."

"Candie might know something about what?" a voice asked from the doorway.

A girl as tall as Tinker but thinner, with a strikingly beautiful face and long, auburn hair, stood in the doorway. "I am incredibly smart, so I probably have the answer. Ask away." She moved into the room and sat down on Tinker's bed.

Maxie recalled the first time they'd met. It was at a rush party, and the girl had been introduced to Maxie and Tinker.

"Candie Barre?" Maxie had whispered later to Tinker. "Is she kidding? Who would name a little kid Candie Barre?"

And from behind her, someone had laughed. "My mother," Candie Barre's voice had said in Maxie's ear. A horrified Maxie had turned around, knowing her face was scarlet, to face the smiling girl. "But it could be worse, right?" the girl had continued. "She could have named me Chocolate. Parents should be forced by law to call their children 'Baby' until the kid is five or six and can pick its own name, right?"

Horribly embarrassed, Maxie had forced a laugh. "You're right. Only a handful of people on this campus know that my real name isn't Maxine. It's Maximilia. Definitely *not* a name I would have picked for myself."

"Well," Candie had said good-naturedly, "now *I* know. But I'll never tell." Maxie had laughed then, and decided she liked this tall, very attractive girl with hair the color of chestnuts.

Tinker had laughed and added, "Well, neither of your names is worse than someone my size being called Tinker." Glancing at Maxie, she had added, "It would sound much better on a shrimp like you."

Maxie glowered. She drew herself up to her full height of five feet, three inches and said indignantly, "I have *stature* that has nothing to do with mere inches! And I have an easier time finding shoes to fit, so there."

When Maxie learned that she had indeed been pledged to Omega Phi, Tinker was the first person she'd shared the news with. But Candie was the second.

Candie loved being an Omega even more than Maxie. Her mother had been president of the sorority in her senior year at Salem, some twenty-two years earlier. "I've been hearing about 'the sisterhood' ever since I was born," she told them, "and I couldn't wait to get here. I was sure my mother was exaggerating. But she wasn't."

Maxie told Candie about Erica's jewelry box.

Horror flooded the pretty face. "You can't mean it's been stolen!" she said in a voice filled with disbelief. "I know other houses and some of the dorms have had some problems with thieves, but not us! Not here!"

"Oh, we don't know that it was stolen," Tinker said quickly. "Maybe it just got . . . misplaced or something."

"Misplaced?" Candie shot her a cynical look. "I've *seen* that box. It wouldn't be easy to misplace. Besides, it's not as if Erica lugs it around with her."

"I don't know about you guys, but I don't want this getting around on campus," Maxie said.

"Oh, of course not," Candie said, her dark eyes wide. "That would be awful! We all have to promise not to tell a soul."

They promised.

But Maxie had a sinking feeling that if the jewelry box really had been stolen, they wouldn't be able to keep it quiet for long. Bad news traveled very fast on campus. And a lot of people who disliked sororities and fraternities would be delighted.

That included Brendan and Jenna. Brendan would curl that gorgeous upper lip of his and say something like, "So someone over there has sticky fingers, eh?" And Jenna would toss her dyed bangs, stick her chubby thumbs in the straps of her coveralls and say, "Nothing like that ever happens at Lester."

Which probably wasn't true at all, but you'd never get Jenna to admit that.

At lunch, Maxie noticed that Erica's eyes were pink-edged. She'd been crying about her grandmother's ring. When she'd finished eating, Maxie offered to help her search. She didn't really expect to find the box downstairs, but they'd already looked throughout the second and third floors, so she began in the living room. She'd just moved on to the kitchen when the doorbell rang.

"I'll get it!" she shouted, and hurried down the hall to the front door.

A young woman in a messenger's uniform stood on the porch. "Package for Erica Bingham," she said, extending a large box wrapped in plain brown paper. With her other hand, she extended a clipboard. "You her?"

"Perfect timing," Maxie murmured. A package might cheer up Erica.

"Excuse me?" The messenger peered at her from behind sunglasses.

"Nothing. No, I'm not her," taking the clipboard, "but I can sign for her."

She signed with a flourish, then closed the door and hurried up the stairs to Erica's room. Knocking on the closed door, she called, "Erica! Package for you."

Erica, her usually calm, composed face twisted with anxiety, yanked the door open.

The room was a disaster. Bedding was upended, drawers tilted open, clothing spilling out, closet doors ajar, books out of bookshelves, sprawled on the floor. In her frantic search, Erica had left nothing untouched.

"What *is* it?" Erica cried impatiently when she saw Maxie.

"I said, you got a package. I brought it right up." Thrusting the box forward, Maxie moved into the room. "Can I . . . can I help you look or help you straighten up or something?" she asked tentatively.

"Who's it from?"

"What?"

"The package. Who's it from?"

Maxie shrugged. "I don't know. No return address. Open it. Maybe it's something wonderful."

Fresh tears dangled on Erica's long eyelashes. "Right. The way my luck is going today, it'll probably explode when I open it." But she placed the package on the bed and began unwrapping it. Her fingers, Maxie noticed, were shaking. Praying there would be something good in the box, something to cheer up Erica, she leaned against the wall and watched as Erica pulled the last sheet of paper away from the contents.

The object inside was large. Rectangular. Shiny black lacquer with pastel flowers dancing across the top.

Erica stood beside the bed, looking down.

"I . . . I don't understand," she whispered. "How . . . ?"

Maxie moved to stand beside her. "What is it?" Then she reached the bed and looked for herself.

The jewelry box. Undamaged. And, as Erica reached out and lifted the lid, apparently not tampered with. The upper, red-velvetted tray was still overflowing with jewelry, including a beautiful pearl ring that Erica immediately snatched up and slid onto her left ring finger, crying out happily, "My grandmother's ring! It's still here!"

Watching her, Maxie smiled with relief. She'd never seen Omega Phi's normally reserved president so elated.

But Maxie's smile didn't last long. In spite of Erica's relief and joy, something wasn't right.

Why would someone take the jewelry box . . . and then return it?

It made no sense.

Chapter 2

With her jewelry box sitting safely on her dresser once again, Erica wanted to forget the whole nasty business. "It must have been a joke," she insisted when Maxie argued.

"Erica," Maxie pointed out, "no one here would find that funny. They wouldn't take something that valuable as a prank."

"Well, what does it matter now, Maxie? I mean, it's over and done with, right? All's well that ends well." Contented, Erica began sifting through her jewelry, making sure that nothing was missing, fingering several rings, fondly letting the necklaces slide through her hands.

Maxie knew a made-up mind when she ran into one. Erica had chosen to put the unpleasant episode out of her mind, as if it had never happened.

But it had.

Giving up, Maxie returned to her room and

sat down on the bed, looking out the wall of windows over the lawn. The house was quiet. Were she and Erica the only ones home?

For the first time since she'd moved, bag and baggage, from Lester into the sorority house, Maxie felt uneasiness tingling her spine. Erica could focus all she wanted to on the fact that the jewelry box had been returned, but Maxie McKeon couldn't help feeling the whole incident was . . . strange.

That night she had dinner with Jenna Dwyer at Burger's Etc., a long, silver diner across the road from campus. She had told Brendan to meet her at the diner later. She wanted to have a couple of hours alone with her ex-roommate.

Guilty conscience, she had told herself when she'd called Lester earlier that afternoon. You haven't had much time for Jenna lately, and you promised yourself when you left the dorm that you'd stay friends.

Jenna Dwyer was the first person Maxie had met on campus. By the time she learned that Jenna hated sororities and fraternities, the two were already friends. "I wouldn't join even if they asked me," Jenna had said when Maxie received her first invitation to a "rush" party. "And trust me, they won't ask."

She was right. Not one sorority sent outspoken Jenna an invitation to a tea or a party or a lunch. They weren't any more interested in her than she was in them. Her wardrobe consisted mainly of ripped jeans, funky tops, and wild, mismatched earrings. She considered high heels a "plot to cripple women," and she had dyed her short, wiry bangs a garish orange-red.

"Definitely not sisterhood material," she had joked while Maxie was packing her bags to leave their room in Lester, and if Maxie thought she heard a note of wistfulness in the comment, she quickly told herself she had to be imagining it. Jenna had made her feelings about sororities perfectly clear. The wistfulness, if it was there at all, had to be because she didn't want Maxie leaving.

The ironic thing, it seemed to Maxie as she saw Jenna loping across the highway toward her, was that Jenna probably could have been pledged if she'd wanted. She might not dress the way the sorority girls did, but she had a great sense of humor and she was smart as a whip. If she'd given Omega Phi half a chance, they might have welcomed her with open arms. An opening had occurred several weeks earlier when one of the girls had had to leave, due to an illness in her family. Maxie could have put

Jenna's name in. She had intended to, and then had decided to ask Jenna first.

Jenna had been horrified. "No way!" she had cried, her big brown eyes open wide. "Leave me out of the sisterhood! They'd make me wear pearls and date someone named Biff. Forget it."

The girl who had been "rushed" instead, and who had eventually decided to pledge the sorority, was Cath Devon, who had been living in an off-campus dorm, Nightingale Hall. She had moved into her room on the third floor the previous Sunday.

Maxie told herself she'd been too busy to get acquainted with Cath, but the truth was, she hadn't yet got over her regret that it was Cath in that room instead of Jenna.

We could have had so much fun, Maxie thought now as she held the diner door open for a cheerful, grinning Jenna. If Ms. Dwyer weren't so darn stubborn . . .

"So, what's up?" Jenna asked as they slid into the only available blue booth. "It's not every Saturday night that I get a call from Omega house. Did they kick you out, I hope? What'd you do, floss your teeth at the table?"

Maxie felt her face flush. She really had to make more time for Jenna. The first few weeks of school would have been a lot harder if Jenna

Dwyer hadn't been there for her.

"I just felt like a hamburger," she said, "and I figured you might, too."

"You don't *look* like a hamburger," Jenna quipped. "And I *don't* feel like one. I'm ordering the taco salad. But I'm still glad you called." Then she added, her brown eyes focused on Maxie's face. "Something *is* up. I can tell. What's wrong? Your new pledgie giving you a hard time? Does she drop the 'g' endings on her words? Wear plaids with stripes? One of *my* favorite wardrobe combinations, by the way. Is she dating a guy in, oh, don't tell me, fine arts instead of the much more desirable premed, prelaw, or business administration programs?" Jenna shook her head in mock despair. Her short, thick blonde hair moved around her cheeks. "Tsk, tsk, when *will* these girls learn?"

Maxie didn't laugh. She knew she shouldn't tell Jenna what had happened. She had promised not to tell. And although no one at Omega house had ever specifically said so, she had a strong feeling that everyone there would frown on her wish to share their bad news with an "outsider."

What was she thinking? Jenna wasn't an "outsider." She was a very good friend.

When they'd given their order to the waitress, Maxie nodded and confessed, "You're right. Something did happen. But it doesn't have anything to do with Cath. She's fine."

"I can't believe I'm saying this," Jenna said, "but I think in Cath's case, moving into a sorority house is definitely a move up, considering where she'd *been* living." She shuddered. "That creepy old house down the road gives me the willies. Always has. I never could figure out why anyone would actually *sleep* there. Or how they *could* sleep there. So dark and gloomy . . . reminds me of the house in *Psycho*."

"Nightingale Hall is pretty creepy," Maxie agreed.

"Nobody calls it Nightingale Hall anymore," Jenna reminded her. "Not since that girl died there. Everyone I know calls it Nightmare Hall now. Makes sense to me."

"I'd forgotten about that girl." Maxie unfolded a white paper napkin on her lap. "I never knew much about it, except that it was all resolved eventually. But Cath told Erica she liked it there. At least, she said she liked the people who live there, especially Jess Vogt, Ian Banion, and Milo Keith. I've seen Cath on campus with Milo."

Their food came, and when Jenna had taken a forkful of salad, chewed, and swallowed, she stuck her fork in the bowl and, leaning forward, said, "You still haven't told me what evil has befallen Omega house. That's an antique, that house. Maybe you've discovered a pre-Civil War ghost hanging out on the third floor?"

Maxie shook her head. "Nothing like that. It's . . . something was . . . taken, that's all."

"Taken?" Jenna looked skeptical. "Am I safe in interpreting that to mean stolen? As in snatched, absconded with, robbed, ripped off?"

"Well, we're not sure."

"Not sure? What, you sorority types don't know what being robbed means?"

"Of course we know. But . . . well, the thing that was taken was . . . returned."

Jenna sank back against the seat. "Ah, a thief suffering pangs of guilt. Shouldn't have gone into that line of work in the first place, if you ask me. Obviously not cut out for it. So, what was snatched? The silverware? TV set?"

"A jewelry box. Erica's jewelry box. But then, a messenger brought it back this afternoon. Weird. Really weird. Who steals things and then sends them back?"

"A thief with a very lenient return policy?" Jenna joked. Then, her voice suddenly serious, she added, "Do you think that someone in the sorority actually stole the thing?"

"Of course not."

"I figured you'd say that. But it's pretty

creepy to think someone came into the house — I mean, don't you lock your doors?"

"Of course we do! Usually. I mean . . ." Maxie's voice weakened . . . "sometimes. I guess sometimes we forget. It's such a nuisance, with people running in and out all day, locking and unlocking all the time."

"Yeah, well, what's really a nuisance," Jenna said as Maxie noticed Brendan entering the diner, "is having *thieves* running in and out all day. Maybe you should think about coming back to Lester, Max. The only people running in and out of the dorm are regular, everyday weirdos like yours truly. Besides," she added quietly, "I *miss* you."

But Maxie was already telling Brendan hi, smiling up at him, and really didn't hear Jenna's final comment. Nor did she see the way Jenna's usual happy expression changed abruptly.

When Brendan and Maxie suggested politely that Jenna tag along to the movies with them, she said, "Oh, wouldn't I just love to be a third wheel. The fact is," she said, flushing slightly, "I have a date. A guy from my chem class. He's no Tom Cruise, but he was incredibly impressed when I told him I intend to be an entomologist. Most people flinch and say, 'A *bug* person? Yuk!' He thought it was neat. So I said yes when he asked me out. We'll do the movie another time, the three of us. Call me."

Someone called out a hello to Brendan then and when he had taken a few steps away from the booth to speak to the friend, Jenna turned to Maxie with concern in her eyes and said, "Listen, think about what I said, okay? I didn't get another roommate after you left. I decided I preferred my privacy. But I make exceptions for exceptional people, so your bed is there whenever you want it back." She turned away, saying over her shoulder, "You shouldn't stay in a place that isn't safe. You don't want the same thing happening to you that happened to that girl at Nightmare Hall."

Maxie felt a cold chill as she watched Jenna hurry away.

Chapter 3

That night, for the first time since she'd moved into Omega house, Maxie slept poorly. She jerked abruptly awake half a dozen times, thinking she'd heard a sound. Each time, although she listened intently, she heard only the silence of a sleeping house and Tinker's deep, even breathing. Each time, it took her a while to drift back into sleep, only to be awakened again a short while later.

She awoke on Sunday morning tired and irritable.

"You'd better cheer up," Tinker warned when Maxie had snapped at her for the third time. "We've got 'The Moms' coming today. We all have to be on our best behavior."

Maxie groaned aloud. The moms! She'd forgotten. Erica's mother, Joan Bingham, an Omega Phi member herself, had rounded up a group of other Omega Phi mothers whose daughters were now in the house, and scheduled a visit for the "first nice Sunday in spring."

"It's not really spring yet," Maxie grumbled, replacing the jeans and sweater she'd planned on wearing, selecting instead a skirt and a white long-sleeved blouse. "And I *don't* feel like being polite and entertaining the moms. I wouldn't think Erica would, either, not after what happened yesterday."

"She probably doesn't. But she can't very well call her mom and cancel at the last minute."

Maxie's mother hadn't been an Omega, but Tinker's mom and Candie's were, and they were planning to make the trip with Erica's mother, and four or five others. "Well," she said grudgingly, "I guess you'll be glad to see your mother. I will, too," she admitted, remembering the warm welcome she'd received when she spent three days at the Gabrielle house during Christmas vacation. "Your mom's okay."

Unfortunately, Maxie had completely forgotten about the visit. All of the girls were expected to be there to welcome the guests and to attend the tea scheduled for that afternoon. But she'd forgotten . . . and had made a date to go canoeing on the river with Brendan that afternoon.

"You'd better call him right now," Tinker suggested. "You know how he hates it when sorority stuff ruins his weekend. The longer you wait, the worse it's going to be."

Taking her advice, Maxie went to the phone.

Calling him right away didn't help that much. "Why didn't you tell me last night?" Brendan asked, clearly irritated.

"I forgot. Erica's mom had been saying for months that they were coming, but we didn't find out that it was this Sunday until this week. I'm sorry. The tea won't last all day. How about a movie tonight?"

His voice was curt. "Maybe. I guess I'll give Jenna a call. Maybe she'd be interested in a canoe ride."

Maxie stared at the receiver in her hand. Jenna? "You're going to take Jenna canoeing?"

"Sure. Why not? We're both taking a back seat to your sorority sisters."

Maxie was speechless. Jenna?

"Look, Maxie," Brendan said into the silence. "I told you when you moved into that house, if sorority life is what you want, fine. Your choice. But I also said that I'm not sitting around doing crossword puzzles while you do your sisterhood thing. Jenna is my friend, too. And I know *she's* not going to any tea this afternoon. Call you later, okay?" And he hung up.

"So?" Tinker asked as she brushed her silvery hair away from her face. "Is he steamed or what?"

"He's steamed. And he says he's going to ask Jenna to go canoeing instead of me."

Tinker put down the brush. "Oh. Well, they're just friends, Maxie. Wipe that I've-just-been-stabbed-in-the-back look off your face. It's just a canoe ride. C'mon, I promised Erica we'd help put those little cucumber sandwiches together before the parental pack arrives."

"I hate cucumbers," Maxie groused. But she slipped into a pair of black flats and followed Tinker downstairs to the kitchen.

Where, as it turned out, they weren't needed. Erica, nervous over the impending arrival of the moms, had summoned a caterer. White uniforms had taken over the kitchen.

Deciding there was no point in hanging around and getting in the way, Maxie grabbed a bag of chips from the pantry and wandered out into the backyard to sit on the low brick wall around the now-empty fountain.

Maxie had only been sitting there a few minutes when half a dozen other Omegas came outside, led by Cath Devon, Candie, and Erica.

"What a pretty yard!" Cath declared, glancing around admiringly. "Nothing like at Nightmare Hall, that's for sure. There must be a gardener, right?"

Maxie nodded and made a face. "Tom Tuttle. Cranky old guy. I'd be perfectly happy to send him off to Nightmare Hall. Gives me the creeps. A couple of the girls have caught him looking in the windows. He always says he's 'washing' them. We must have the cleanest windows in town."

Several other girls joined them then, all dressed in skirts or dresses for the upcoming tea.

"Hey, Candie, guess who called a few minutes ago?" a girl named Chloe called as she approached the fountain.

"Who?"

"Your not-so-secret admirer, Graham Lucas."

Candie groaned. Graham Lucas was a sophomore, not bad-looking, but far too needy and clinging for Candie's tastes. Unfortunately, Candie was to *his* taste, and although she'd told him more than once that she already had a boyfriend, he'd been making a pest of himself lately, calling and sending notes and flowers to the house. Everyone in the house knew what a total pain he was to Candie.

"What did you tell him?" Candie asked as the girls took seats on the fountain wall.

Chloe laughed. "I told him you'd been kidnapped by aliens and hadn't been seen for days."

The others laughed, but Candie frowned. "He didn't laugh, *did* he?"

Chloe's smile disappeared. "No. He didn't. He mumbled something nasty and hung up."

"The guy was born without a sense of humor," Candie said. And then, firmly, "And I don't want to talk about him anymore. Too depressing. If he keeps it up, I'm going straight to security and complain. Now, about my mother, who is even as I speak on her way here. . . ."

She spent the next fifteen minutes telling them stories about her mother's days at Omega house, ending with a warning. "That's all she's going to talk about, so you'll just have to put up with it," she said, adding anxiously, "Does my hair look okay? That's the first thing she'll notice."

Although everyone assured her that her hair looked "just fine," Candie sat there a few more minutes and then, too restless to sit still, went back inside to "do something about this hair."

Half an hour later, Maxie went inside and was heading for the living room when the front door burst open and a tall, thin woman in a full-length fur coat, her bright red hair cut very short, cried, "Darlings! We're here! Oh, it's grand to be *home*! Now, where is my darling Candie?"

Definitely, Maxie thought, a woman who would name a baby "Candie Barr."

Tinker came down the stairs just then. She and Maxie exchanged an amused glance. Although the hair was different, the face was definitely the same face that graced many photos hanging in the upstairs hall. This was Allison Barre, former president of Omega Phi Delta, and mother of Candie.

Following Allison Barre into the house were half a dozen other mothers, including Erica's mother, Joan Bingham. Tall, like her daughter, but thinner, she had graying hair and walked with a slight limp.

As the other mothers filed in and greeted their daughters, Maxie ran upstairs to get Candie. "Your mom's here," she said in the open doorway to Candie's room.

Candie turned away from the mirror. Her face was flushed, her eyes bright. "I know. I heard her. Who didn't? I'm surprised Jenna didn't call you from Lester and say, 'So, Candie's mom arrived okay.'"

Maxie laughed. "She's a powerhouse, all

right. You'd better get downstairs."

"I can't do a thing with my hair," Candie wailed. "She'll hate it, I know she will! She'll insist on sending Tia Maria to see me. That's her hairdresser. Tia Maria!" Candie made a face. "The woman's real name is Gert Tolan. I guess she didn't think that was fancy enough for a beautician with a high-priced clientele." She looked into the mirror and wailed again. "My mother's going to *hate* my hair!"

"No, she's not. It looks great." Maxie grinned. "Wait till you see hers."

Relaxing a little, Candie returned the grin. "What color is it this time?"

"Red. Very, very red."

"Interesting." As they left the room, Candie said urgently, "Listen, don't say anything to my mom about Erica's jewelry box, okay? I'm not sure how she'd react, but I promise you it wouldn't be good. To hear her tell it, nothing bad ever happened when *she* was here. Every moment was a golden one, every day a joy, every night an adventure." Candie sighed. "I don't think she's ever been as happy as she was then." Then she grinned again. "Me, I'm still waiting for the adventurous nights."

"Darling!" her mother shrieked as Candie reached the foot of the stairs, with Maxie right behind her. "What have you done with your hair? It's much too long, sweetie." She whirled in front of Candie. "How do you like mine? Isn't it smashing? Two hundred dollars, and worth every penny of it, don't you think? Listen, I can have Tia Maria call you if you'd like. I'm sure she could make a side trip over here and do yours. Just tip her heavily, darling." Her words came out at machine-gun speed, as if she had no need to take a breath.

Tinker joined Maxie at the foot of the stairs as Allison Barre took her daughter's hand and, still raving about the miracles worked by her hairdresser, led her away. "I can't believe she's anybody's mother," Tinker whispered to Maxie. "Except for the hair, they look like sisters, don't they? But Allison is so . . . so . . ."

"*So*. Period," Maxie agreed. "Can you imagine growing up with that? No milk and cookies there, I'll bet. Caviar and Perrier, probably. No wonder Mrs. Barre is divorced. What man could live with her?"

Erica suggested they all gather in the living room to "become acquainted" before eating.

Maxie sat with Tinker and her mother, watching the other mothers and wondering, Is this what we're going to be like twenty years from now? Like Candie's mother, vibrant and overpowering? Or like Erica's mother, also a past president? Tall and slim and smartly dressed, Joan Bingham seemed to have nothing good to say about anything. Erica flushed repeatedly as her mother criticized the color of the wall paint, the upholstery on the furniture, and Erica's clothes and hair.

Maxie felt sorrier for Erica than she did for Candie. Candie's mother might be hard to live up to, but at least she seemed like fun. Joan Bingham was no day at the beach.

It was a relief when Erica suggested a walk on the grounds.

When they had all gone outside, Maxie, who found herself suddenly missing her own mother, went into the kitchen to see if Mildred needed any help.

The kitchen was empty. Dishes, silverware, and napkins had been set out on the counter, ready to be taken into the dining room, but Mildred was nowhere to be seen.

Deciding to get a Coke and join the others outside, Maxie yanked open the door of the huge white refrigerator.

And was greeted by an overpowering stench that took her breath away.

Gasping, she stared at the white shelves in front of her.

Instead of the plastic-covered trays of prepared food she had been expecting to see, every shelf was filled to overflowing with rotting fruits and vegetables, broken eggshells, wet coffee grounds, crumpled plastic bags and soda bottles, and the bony carcasses of several large chickens or turkeys.

Maxie's mouth dropped open. "Uh . . ." was all she could manage. The putrid smell made her eyes water, but her arm felt frozen in place, preventing her from slamming the refrigerator shut upon the foul mess.

Someone had replaced their perfectly arranged, plastic-covered party trays with a mountain of foul-smelling garbage.

Chapter 4

Maxie stared in horror at the disgusting mess overflowing on the refrigerator shelves. When, one hand pinching her nostrils closed against the smell, she leaned closer, she saw no sign of the neatly wrapped trays for the tea. They had disappeared.

She sagged against the refrigerator door.

"Maxie, close that door! You're wasting electricity," Erica's voice said from behind Maxie's shoulder.

Maxie turned to stare at her with sickened eyes.

"Maxie? What's wrong?"

Maxie moved aside to let Erica see.

When the full effect of the sight and smell had hit her, Erica's hand flew up to cover her mouth and nose. "Oh, no," she breathed. "Our tea . . ." and then, her face draining of color, "oh, God, if my mother sees this. . . !"

But she recovered quickly. Turning, she ran to the phone to summon the caterer back to the house. "Keep everyone out of the kitchen," she whispered frantically to Maxie as she dialed. "Don't let *anyone* in, especially my mother. Make a speech, do a song-and-dance routine, stand on your head, I don't care what you do, but *keep* them out of this room!"

Still stunned and shaken, Maxie returned to the living room, where everyone had just returned from their walk. Joan Bingham, Erica's mother, sat alone in a corner, complaining loudly about being "famished" and asking repeatedly where her daughter was. Candie's mother sat in the center of the room. The subject of her humorous stories had switched from her hairdresser to her own past, some twenty-two years ago, at Omega house.

I'll bet, Maxie thought numbly as she joined the group, she's *not* going to say that back then things were stolen out of the rooms, or that one day they found the refrigerator shelves piled high with smelly garbage.

How had that happened? Why would someone *do* something so ugly? *When* had they done it? Had to have been after the caterer's staff left. The kitchen would have been deserted, at least for a little while.

Maxie glanced around the room, wondering

why no one saw in her face that she was upset. Was she that good an actress? Or was it just that everyone was raptly listening to Allison Barre, who spoke of sorority life with great affection and enthusiasm.

"It was perfect," Allison said wistfully, "absolutely perfect. The four happiest years of my life." Then she remembered Candie and added hastily, "Until my darling daughter here came along, of course." Candie flushed as her mother patted her hand. "And now she's getting *her* chance to have the most wonderful time of her life. And you know, it doesn't end when you leave school. Your sisterhood goes on forever. Sorority activities still keep me very, very busy. These lovely girls, Candie," glancing around the room approvingly, "will be a part of your life even when you're old and gray, right, Joan?"

Erica's mother drew her lips together in a thin, straight line. "Doesn't look to me like *you* ever intend to *be* gray, Allie. All I know is when *we* were here," Mrs. Bingham added disapprovingly, "tea was served on *time*."

"Oh, Joan, lighten up! Have a cracker or something." Dismissing Joan Bingham, Allison began a new story about a dance held at the house when she was president.

Maxie wasn't listening. She was watching

out the living room window for the caterer's truck.

Tinker came over and sat on the floor beside Maxie's chair. "You okay?" she asked. "You look like you just witnessed an autopsy." Tinker was premed.

So, I'm *not* that great an actress, was Maxie's reaction. No wonder I wasn't in drama in high school like just about everybody else in this room. She was suddenly very grateful to Allison Barre. If the woman hadn't had everyone so enthralled, they'd all be asking Maxie what was wrong. And what would she say?

"Tell you later," she answered briefly, and saw the caterer's truck pull into the driveway. Had Erica had time to remove the disgusting mess in the frig? She'll have to give the caterer some reason for all that work being useless, Maxie thought. Would she tell the truth?

But she knew even as she thought it that Erica wouldn't. She'd invent some story for the disaster, knowing that the caterer served other sorority houses as well as their own, and that people were more likely to pass on bad news than good. Omega Phi's president wouldn't be willing to take that chance.

Maxie hurried into the kitchen.

The small catering staff was already bustling about in the kitchen, dour looks on their faces.

A large black plastic bag, bulging at the seams and pinched at the neck by a twist-tie, leaned against the back door. Erica must have done a thorough job, Maxie thought as she offered to help.

A tall, thin woman in white nodded. "You can take those plates in," she said, and muttered something under her breath.

As Maxie picked up the plates, she murmured to Erica, who was gathering a handful of silverware, "If she'd brought the whole staff back, it would go faster."

"She did bring the whole staff back," Erica whispered. "That's what she's complaining about. She has to pay them all double time." She sighed. "So, of course, we're going to have to pay *her* twice, too. After all, that mess in the frig wasn't *her* fault."

"She did not bring the whole staff back," Maxie disagreed as the two headed for the dining room with their burdens. "There's one missing. That older woman with gray hair. Reminded me of my Aunt Minnie. She was in the pantry when I was downstairs earlier."

Erica frowned. "There wasn't any older woman, Max. There were only three of them, and none of them had gray hair."

Maxie shook her head. "I *saw* her, Erica." She set the plates on a corner of the dining room table. "She was wearing white, just like the others."

"I don't know who you saw, Maxie, but it wasn't a member of the catering staff."

Then the food was brought in, everyone was invited into the dining room, and Maxie was left wondering if she could have imagined the elderly woman in white in the pantry.

She hadn't actually seen the woman's face. When she had entered the pantry to grab a bag of chips, the woman was standing with her back to the door. Maxie had said hello, and although the woman had answered pleasantly enough, she hadn't turned around. Her face had been aimed toward the shelves and wasn't visible. Maxie had seen a white uniform, gray hair worn in a bun, covered with a hair net, and a pair of sensible white shoes like her Aunt Minnie, a nurse, wore.

But she hadn't seen the woman's face.

If you were standing somewhere and someone came up behind you and said hello, wouldn't you automatically turn your head to see who it was?

Sure you would.

Maxie took a seat at the table, between Candie and Joan Bingham, who was complaining loudly about the delay. "When *I* lived in this house," she said in a thin, high-pitched voice, "the teas we held were served at four o'clock sharp." She directed a disapproving glance at her red-faced daughter, seated on her right.

"It couldn't be helped, Mother," Erica said meekly. "I'm sorry. After you came all this way . . ."

Maxie glanced at Erica in surprise. She sounded so totally unlike herself. They were all used to Erica making plans in a voice that was self-confident and optimistic. This Erica, so apologetic, so embarrassed, was foreign to all of them.

"It wasn't Erica's fault," Maxie couldn't help saying. "Something — "

She had been about to say, "Something happened," when Erica cut her off sharply, silencing Maxie with a desperate look.

"It's nothing," Erica said hastily, passing her mother a basket of rolls. "Really, I just screwed up. I apologize to everyone. Now, let's just enjoy, okay?"

Joan Bingham fell silent and began eating, to everyone's relief, and after a tense, uneasy moment or two, everyone else did the same.

Erica is scared to death that her mother will find out what really happened, Maxie told herself, wielding a butter knife with an expert touch. She could get herself off the hook so easily by telling her mother the truth. No one could blame Erica for what happened in the kitchen. Why isn't she being honest?

She asked Erica that, the first chance she had. The mothers had left, and everyone else had scattered to their rooms to get ready for dates or to study. Maxie found Erica in the kitchen, sweeping the floor.

"Erica," she began, "why didn't you tell anyone about the frig? You let everyone think you screwed up, and you *didn't*."

"You mean I let my *mother* think I screwed up," Erica said, continuing to sweep. "And you can't figure out why I would do that, when she was so obviously irritated, right?"

Maxie nodded. "Right. What happened wasn't your fault. She couldn't have blamed you for that mess on the shelves."

Erica stopped sweeping. She leaned against the counter. The expression on her square, attractive face was serious as she addressed Maxie in a low voice. "I know you think my mother is a shrew," she said. "Everyone does."

Before Maxie could protest, Erica added quickly, "But she wasn't always like that. Like you saw her today, I mean. She used to be tons of fun, happy and laughing, like Candie's mother. I know she was really popular in college, and that always made sense to me, because she was so . . . so *fun*." The blue eyes were full of regret as Erica added, "But when my dad died, she changed. Became overprotective. Because I'm all she's got left, I guess. Calls me all the time, writes constantly, nagging me about dressing properly and taking vitamins, that kind of stuff. So," Erica resumed sweeping again, her movements careless and absentminded, "if she knew that something had been taken from my room, and then returned, if she knew about the mess in the frig, she'd yank me out of this house, yank me out of college, probably. Make me come home and live with her, where I'd be 'safe.'" Erica's shoulders moved in a shudder. "I couldn't stand that."

Maxie ran a hand through her dark curls. Her mind fought against Erica's words. "You don't think this house is safe?" Jenna had implied the same thing. But Erica . . . Erica was Omega Phi's *president*. If *she* didn't believe they were safe . . .

Erica stopped sweeping again to glance at Maxie. "Someone," she said slowly, carefully, "has been in this house twice in the past week. Someone who had no business being here. Someone who was up to no good. Does that sound safe to you, Maxie?"

Chapter 5

As she returned to her room, Maxie thought about what Erica had said. She was overreacting, wasn't she? It wasn't as if anyone had been *hurt*. No poison in their cucumber sandwiches, no knife-wielding maniac running up and down the halls, no one had been thrown down the wide, curving stairs with the thick wooden railing.

Maxie jumped when the phone shrilled. Then, shaking herself sternly, she picked up the receiver.

It was Brendan.

"Where are you?" she asked abruptly.

"I'm at Vinnie's. I thought you might like to meet me for pizza."

"Is Jenna with you?" Maxie had to ask.

"Jenna? No. She had a paper to write, so she headed for the library. Why?"

Their canoe ride hadn't led to anything else.

Good. "No reason. I just wondered." She was suddenly starving. She hadn't eaten much at the tea.

Maxie took the local shuttle bus to Vinnie's, a favorite pizza hangout, which was only a few minutes from campus. Brendan was sitting alone in a booth at the back when Maxie walked in. When they had ordered, she told him about the strange things that had been happening at Omega house.

When their pizza arrived, hot and gooey, Brendan was still trying to make sense of it. "I don't get it," he said, carefully picking up a slice of tomatoey crust. "Someone stole something but gave it back? Someone filled your frig with garbage?"

Maxie nodded.

"Maybe it's that creepy gardener of yours," Brendan suggested. "Sounds like the kind of stunt he'd pull to rattle your cages. Did anyone check him out before they hired him?"

"Tom Tuttle? Mildred probably did. Or the university. Anyway, he's creepy, but I haven't seen him inside the house, and if Erica had, she'd have told me. And why would Tom Tuttle take something from one of the rooms and then send it back by messenger?"

Brendan shrugged and wiped tomato sauce from his mouth with a paper napkin. "Why would anyone? Just to let you know they'd been in the house, I guess. Like I said, to rattle your cage."

"That's mean. I don't know anyone that creepy."

"Sure you do. We all do. We just don't know it, because they're creepy enough to hide it." Brendan smiled the smile that had won Maxie's heart. "Creepy people don't walk around with signs hanging around their necks saying, 'Don't trust me, I'm creepy.' "

Maxie laughed, and reached for a slice of pizza.

"So," Brendan said casually, "you going to move back to the dorm or what?"

"I'm not moving anywhere," Maxie said firmly, taking a healthy bite of cheese-and-tomato-sauced crust. "Omega house is where I live now. No one's chasing me out with some stupid stunts."

"Then you'd better think about tightening security around that place," Brendan said, his voice grim. "You just told me someone's been getting into the place without anyone raising an eyebrow. Maybe he's just pulling 'stupid stunts' now, but if you don't do something to keep him out, who knows what he'll do next?"

Maxie put her pizza back on her plate. Brendan sounded just like Jenna. "Who knows what he'll do next?" Wasn't that exactly what Erica had been afraid to say out loud?

Seeing that he had upset her, Brendan added quickly, "It's probably someone you guys didn't let into the inner sanctum. You know, someone who didn't make it into Omega Phi. I guess that's worse than death to some girls, crazy as that sounds. I don't get it, myself. What's the big deal about some silly Greek letters."

Maxie toyed with a fork as Brendan's suggestion registered. "Someone we rushed and then didn't accept?"

"There must be a whole bunch of girls on this campus you guys didn't take," Brendan said. "Maybe one of them is a lot unhappier about it than the others. She could be out to make you all as miserable as you made her."

Maxie thought about that for a moment. Two girls in particular came to mind: Isabella Sands and Holly Dukes. Both had been shocked when they hadn't made it into Omega Phi, and neither had made any secret of her feelings. Isabella had accosted Maxie on campus, angrily questioning her, and Holly had phoned Erica more than once to demand an explanation. But Isabella had a nasty disposition and a habit of spreading rumors about people, while Holly was painfully shy, almost withdrawn. Still, she had seemed very determined to become an Omega Phi Delta.

Maxie had heard that the vote was unanimous in both cases. Not Omega Phi material.

I got in and they didn't, Maxie thought now. Am I going to pay for that?

Brendan insisted on driving her back to the house in his car. Maxie had an uneasy feeling that he didn't want her going back to Omega house alone.

Tomorrow she would ask Erica about Tom Tuttle. How long had he worked at Omega house? Where had he come from? He didn't have a criminal record, did he?

She could only hope that Erica would have the answers to those questions.

And maybe it wouldn't hurt to talk to Isabella and Holly, too. See if they still seemed as angry about being rejected by the sorority of their choice. She already knew they hadn't been pledged to any other sorority. They were both still living at Lester, one floor above Jenna.

"Look," Brendan said solemnly before he kissed her good night, "I don't want to get all crazed about this, but if this funny business keeps up, promise me you'll think about moving back to Lester, okay? At least until this stuff blows over? Jenna has room for you. She didn't get a new roommate yet."

The two of them had talked about her? Maxie flushed angrily, and her good-night kiss was cooler than usual.

Brendan didn't seem to notice. "See you to-morrow," he said. "Lock your door, okay?" And he loped down the steps and over to his car, where he stopped and watched to make sure she was safely inside. Only then did he leave.

The house was quiet, the big living room empty, the television off. Muted sounds of music and conversation and running water floated down from upstairs. The weekend was winding down. Her sisters were getting ready for the new week.

Maxie sighed as she started up the wide, curving staircase. This week *had* to be better than the weekend.

She stopped in to see Erica before going to her own room. The sorority president was lying on her bed, but she sat up when Maxie entered. Her face was very pale and strained-looking.

"Tinker thought we should call the police," she said as Maxie sat down on the bed beside her. "But I hate that idea. We've never had them here before. We can handle this our-selves, at least for now."

"Brendan thinks maybe it's someone we rejected. Someone we didn't pledge."

Horror filled Erica's square, strong face. "You told Brendan? Maxie, how *could* you? I thought we agreed to keep this quiet! Do you want every sorority on campus gossiping about us?"

"He won't tell anyone," Maxie said with more confidence than she felt. He wouldn't, would he? Maybe Jenna . . . so they could both agree that Maxie was foolish to stay at Omega house. Feeling suddenly disloyal to Brendan, she quickly added, "Besides, Erica, maybe he's got a point. It *could* be someone we turned down. Someone who's angry with us."

Calming down, Erica nodded. "Maybe you're right. I'll go over the list tomorrow. Maybe I'll talk to those girls, sound them out. See if I can tell if any of them might be angry enough to sneak in here and try to get even with us." Then she added thoughtfully, "Some people don't take rejection well at all."

Feeling much better, as she always did when action was being taken, Maxie said good night and headed back to her own room.

But as she passed Candie's room, the door standing open, she saw Candie standing in the middle of the room, her hands clasped together, tears streaming down her cheeks, wet hair spilling over her shoulders.

Maxie's first reaction was, Oh, no, what now? But then Candie became her concern, and she hurried over to her roommate's side. "Candie? What's wrong?"

"My ring is gone. The ring Dylan gave me." Candie's boyfriend, Dylan Pierce, was miles away at an Ivy League college, but they kept in constant touch by mail and phone. Maxie knew the ring, a plain gold band with Candie's birthstone, a tiny ruby, set in the center, was the most important piece of jewelry Candie owned. The only time it left the ring finger of her left hand was when she showered. She was terrified that it would slip off her hand and disappear down a watery drain.

"I left it on my bedside table like I always do when I shower," she said tearfully, pointing with a shaking finger toward the table in question. "And when I came back out, it was gone." She stared at Maxie with tear-filled eyes. "Gone!" she breathed, as if she couldn't quite believe it.

"Calm down," Maxie said, in spite of a coil of dread that was spiraling upward inside of her. "I'll help you look." But she didn't really expect to find the ring.

And they didn't. Although they searched everywhere, it was nowhere to be seen. It hadn't fallen off the table and landed in the carpeting, it hadn't rolled behind the picture frames and books and notebooks on Candie's table, and it wasn't lying underneath the sink in the bathroom.

Candie's beloved ring had disappeared.

And all Maxie could think was, it's happening again.

Chapter 6

The next morning, Maxie and Candie were the last to arrive in the kitchen. Everyone else had already left the house for classes. When they had eaten, they approached Mildred, asking if anyone who didn't belong in the house had been there the previous evening. Since Erica had already told the housemother about the jewelry box, they also told her about Candie's ring.

Mildred was horrified. When she was finally convinced that Candie hadn't simply misplaced the ring, she said, "Well, let me see. The mothers were here. And the caterers were here twice. But they'd never steal anything. And Tom came in for a few minutes yesterday, to empty some garbage. But of course, he *does* belong here, so he wouldn't count."

When no one said anything, Mildred added slowly, "I'm as reluctant to call in the police as Erica is. Nasty business, having police cars come to the house. But if you haven't found it by tomorrow morning, Candace, we'll have no choice. We'll have to summon them. Was the ring very valuable?"

Fresh tears filled Candie's eyes. "Only to me, I guess." Sadly she turned around and left for class.

Thinking that she had never seen Candie look so upset, Maxie went upstairs to shower.

She had just come down the stairs, books in hand, when the doorbell rang. Maxie answered the ring, to find a gray-haired man dressed in a white doctor's coat standing on the porch. He was holding a large white handkerchief to his face. It was dotted with blotches of dark red. Maxie noticed a large black medical bag dangling from his free hand.

"Sorry to bother you," he said from behind the handkerchief, "but my car cut out on me just around the corner. I was wondering if I might use your phone to call a tow truck."

"You're hurt," Maxie said, pulling the door open and waving him inside. "You didn't have an accident?"

"No, miss." The man laughed. "I'm due at your infirmary for a consultation, and I was already late. Got so steamed when my car quit, I jumped out without looking and ran into a low-hanging tree limb. I need to call over there and tell them I'll be late, and I need to get my car off that street corner before your campus security sees it and tows it." Keeping the handkerchief over his nose and mouth gave his words a high, nasal quality. He put down his medical bag and extended a hand toward Maxie. "Michael Clark," he said. "Dr. Michael Clark."

"Are you sure you're okay?" Maxie asked, shaking the man's hand. "You're bleeding."

"It's just a nosebleed. Could I borrow your phone?"

"Of course. And I'm sure it will be all right if you wait here for the tow truck. I have to leave, but our housemother, Mildred Booth, should be around here somewhere."

He waved a hand in dismissal. "Thanks. You go ahead. I'll be fine."

Worried that he might not be as okay as he insisted he was, Maxie went looking for Mildred. Failing to find her, she went back into the living room, unsure of what she should do.

The doctor was talking on the telephone. Deciding that he seemed to have the situation in hand and that Mildred was probably out back and would return momentarily, Maxie left for campus.

Concentrating on her classes wasn't easy. When she wasn't thinking of Candie and the missing ring, she was thinking of the injured doctor. Maybe she shouldn't have left him. What if he had a concussion or something?

Maxie, a voice argued, he's a *doctor*. He would certainly know if he had a concussion, wouldn't he? He told you he didn't need you, so he didn't need you. Period. Her thoughts turned to Tom Tuttle. Mildred had said he'd been in the house the day before. Had he emptied that garbage onto the refrigerator shelves?

Why would old Tom Tuttle take Erica's jewelry box and Candie's ring?

"I heard about Candie's ring," Tinker said as they stood in line at the student center's lunch counter. "She must be really upset."

Maxie nodded. "She is."

Tinker shook her head. "I can't believe this kind of stuff is happening at Omega house. Can you?"

"No," Maxie admitted.

They sat at a corner table. Maxie was unwrapping her sandwich when Candie joined them.

"You guys look like you lost your best friends. I'm the one who lost something, remember?"

"We were just talking about that," Tinker said. "Did you call your mom and tell her the ring was missing?"

Candie looked skeptical. "Are you kidding? I didn't tell her about Erica's jewelry box, either. Because she'd never believe me, not in a zillion years."

"Well, of course she would," Tinker said. "She knows you wouldn't lie about something like that."

"Nope." Candie shook her head. "Not at the Omega Phi Delta house, in which Allison Barre spent the happiest years of her life." She lifted a forkful of pie. "My mother has tunnel vision where her sorority is concerned. She only sees the good, and she won't tolerate hearing anything bad about it."

"It's your sorority, too, Candie," Maxie pointed out gently.

"Yeah, I know." Candie tossed her chestnut-colored hair. "And it's nice to have that in common with her. Something we share. It's fun. Especially now with my dad and my brother gone. Enough about that," Candie said. "Are we still going to have Cath walk the wall tonight?"

Each sorority had its own rituals to initiate a new member. At Omega Phi, the very last of these, which Cath Devon had not yet performed, was a blindfolded walk around the brick wall surrounding the fountain.

"I don't know," Maxie answered, shrugging.

"I guess so. I had forgotten about it. All I want right now is for your ring to show up, Candie."

And show up, it did.

It was Maxie who, once again, answered the door. She had come home from classes to find the house empty, Mildred gone, a note on the kitchen bulletin board announcing that the housemother had gone into town and would "be back soon." Maxie was helping herself to a handful of grapes when the doorbell rang.

She knew before she even opened the door, with an eerie sense of certainty, that it was a messenger.

It was. The same one as the first time. She smiled as she handed Maxie the small package. "For Candace Barre," she said, and grinned. "Candie Barre? Far out." Then she handed Maxie the clipboard to sign.

The package was so small, Maxie knew it had to be the gold ring with the ruby in the center.

"Who sent you?" she asked quickly as the messenger turned to leave.

The young woman frowned. "Triple-A Messenger Services," she said, pointing to the label embroidered on her jacket pocket. Her tone implied, Can't you read?

"I mean," Maxie amended awkwardly, "do

you know where this package came from? Who sent it?"

"Nope. I just deliver them. She *does* live here, doesn't she?"

Maxie nodded. "I'll see that she gets it."

The messenger left then. Maxie stood watching as the young woman ran down the steps and jumped on the bicycle waiting at the base of the hill.

Erica's jewelry box had been taken . . . and returned.

Now Candie's ring had arrived back at Omega house.

On the one hand, it was wonderful for Candie. On the other hand, it meant that the person who had taken Erica's jewelry box hadn't had an attack of conscience, after all. It meant that returning the box was simply part of the game he or she was playing. Toying with them, jerking them around, he the puppetmaster, they the puppets, dancing to his tune.

The game hadn't ended. Not yet.

The puppetmaster was still jerking their strings.

Chapter 7

Candie was ecstatic when she ripped the wrapping off the package Maxie had given her and discovered the ring inside. She yanked the ring from the box and waved it in the air, grinning from ear to ear. "I can't believe it!" she cried. "Where did you get it?"

"Delivered by messenger," Maxie answered grimly. "Just like Erica's jewelry box." As much as she hated to ruin Candie's joy, she couldn't let the matter rest there. "Candie, I don't like this at all. Maybe it's just a game, maybe it isn't. But the fact is, someone has been getting into our rooms." She had a sudden mental image of a dark figure sneaking into Candie's room, glancing about with sly eyes, moving stealthily to the table, picking up the ring, pocketing it . . . she shuddered.

Candie slipped the ring onto her finger. "Well, the ring is back on my finger where it belongs. That's all I care about. And maybe that's it for now, right? Nothing else will be taken and we can forget about this nasty stuff."

"I hope you're right." Maxie got up to leave. Erica had decided that since the weather was good, tonight would be a good time to hold the final ceremony that would make Cath Devon a full-fledged member of Omega Phi Delta. The new pledge would perform her blindfolded walk around the brick fountain wall after dinner. "If Cath realizes that weirdos are waltzing in and out of our rooms taking things, she'll pack her bags and go running back to Nightmare Hall so fast, she'll be a blur on the highway."

Lost in the joy of retrieving her precious ring, Candie didn't answer.

Maxie went back to her room, changed into a skirt and sweater and was about to go looking for Mildred to find out what had happened with the injured doctor, when the phone rang. Tinker walked into the room just as Maxie picked up the receiver.

It was Jenna calling. "The campus movie to-night is Elvis!" she screeched into the phone. Jenna was obsessed with Elvis Presley. Her room was plastered with Elvis photos and she had even taken a trip to Graceland. "We have *got* to go! Meet me in front at seven."

She would have hung up then, but Maxie said

quickly, "Jenna, I can't. Cath's walking the wall tonight."

There was a moment of stunned silence. Then, the excitement gone from her voice, Jenna said, "Ah, yes, the famous wall-walk. Wouldn't want to miss that, would you? Must be right up there with catching the fireworks on the Fourth of July or watching the ball descend in Times Square on New Year's Eve. A silly old Elvis movie must pale in comparison. Sorry I asked."

Stung, and feeling guilty, Maxie retorted, "It's just a tradition, Jenna. Like . . . like going caroling at Christmas or dressing up at Halloween. *You* dress up at Halloween."

"I'm sure it's *exactly* like that." Jenna's voice reeked of sarcasm. Then, more casually, she added, "Well, maybe I'll call Brendan."

"Brendan doesn't like Elvis movies."

"Maybe not. But since you're too busy for *him*, too, maybe he'll decide a movie is better than nothing. See you." And she hung up.

Maxie stared at the receiver in her hand. She and Jenna had had this argument before.

It was so hard to make people who didn't belong, like Brendan and Jenna, understand that she took her sorority seriously.

And now, when she needed her friends' support, their answer was for her to move back to

Lester. And that wasn't what she wanted.

"Jenna mad again?" Tinker asked, brushing her short, pale hair away from her face.

Maxie nodded.

"She'll get over it. She always does."

Maybe, Maxie thought. But did Jenna really "get over it"? Or did she just bury her anger somewhere until she needed it again?

Would Brendan go to that movie with Jenna?

"Candie and I are responsible for the food tonight," Maxie told Tinker. "I'd better go find her and get things started. See you outside."

As she walked along the wide, carpeted upstairs hallway to Candie's room, she couldn't help wondering how someone, a stranger, could have wandered the halls of Omega house, slipping in and out of rooms, taking things, without being seen. Had he been watching the house, waiting for hours until the moment when it was completely empty?

Gruesome thought, the idea of being watched.

The house was not completely empty very often. So many girls, going different places at different times. They all seldom left the house at the same time. And when they weren't there, Mildred usually was. How had the sneak thief got past Mildred?

Erica's refusal to call in the police suddenly

62

seemed foolish . . . maybe even dangerous. Unless Candie was right, and there would be no more thefts.

She collected Candie and they went downstairs together.

Although the overhead fluorescent light was on, the large, square white room seemed deserted. Mildred wasn't there, puttering at the sink or the fat, white stove or refrigerator. Plates and silverware and a thick pile of folded white napkins sat on the blue kitchen counter, in preparation for the dinner that would take place following the ceremony. Blue ceramic candleholders and white candles sat next to the dishes.

The room was so still, so quiet, that when a noise came from the walk-in pantry, Maxie jumped. And then relaxed. Silly girl. Mildred wasn't in the kitchen because she was in the pantry, collecting some last-minute items for the ceremony.

"Well," Maxie told Candie, "we came to help, so let's help."

They walked over to the pantry door and Maxie pulled it open.

But the light wasn't on. All she could see at first was a bulky figure standing in front of the shelves. It wasn't Mildred. Too short, too wide. Not Mildred at all.

Her heart began pounding in her chest. What was someone who wasn't Mildred doing in the pantry in total darkness?

She took a step backward, smacking into Candie, who let out an "oof" sound. "Who's there?" Maxie called into the deep, wide pantry. "What are you doing in there?"

"Jus gettin' a can of beans," the voice of the gardener answered. "Miz Booth said I could."

Maxie let out a long breath of air. It was only the gardener, Tom Tuttle, in the pantry.

"In the dark?" Maxie questioned skeptically. "How can you find a can of anything in there without a light?"

"Got my flashlight," came the answer. "Don't need it, though. I know where Miz Booth keeps the beans."

An arm reached up in the dark, lifted something off a shelf, and turned to begin approaching Maxie.

She backed up another step or two, pushing Candie along with her.

When he reached the doorway, the man fastened pale, watery eyes on Maxie and said sullenly, "I wasn't stealin' nothin'. You can ask Miz Booth." He held up the red-labeled can of beans. "She *said* I could have this. Go ahead, *ask* her if you don't believe me."

He had a mean set to his mouth, Maxie

thought, and he needed a shave. "I believe you," she said, anxious to be rid of him. "Why wouldn't I?"

He lowered his grizzled head. "I know what goes on here. I know some things been missin'. I seen the way you people look at me, like I'm not as good as you."

"That's not true," Maxie protested feebly. But she thought maybe it was.

"But I didn't take nothin'," Tom Tuttle said vehemently, his eyes still on the floor. "Only the stuff Miz Booth says I can have. And I don't want nobody sayin' nothin' different." And without lifting his head, he shuffled away from the two girls and went out the back door, slamming it loudly behind him.

"I don't think I'd want him really mad at me," Candie said softly. "He has mean eyes."

Maxie nodded. Then she added slowly, "We don't really look at him like he said, do we? Like we're better than he is?"

"Probably." Candie switched on the pantry light. It wasn't very bright, providing only a dim yellowish glow. "But if we do, it's just because he's, well, he's not very clean and he's a grouch. And he peeks in the windows sometimes, we all know that. We should get rid of him, but Erica says he's been here forever. Like Mildred."

Maxie and Candie moved on into the pantry, grateful that it was no longer pitch-black inside. It took only a second or two to locate the things they'd need for dinner. Maxie reached out a hand for one of the boxes.

It moved.

Maxie gasped. "What . . . ?" she murmured, staring at the round container.

And then she saw that the container wasn't actually moving at all. Something . . . a *lot* of somethings . . . were moving *on* it. Black things. Large, elongated, dark things . . . *living* things, were crawling all over the box.

Maxie's arm flew back to her side. *"Candie,"* she whispered. *"Look . . ."*

Candie looked. And cried out. *"What? What is that?"*

Maxie's heart rose into her throat as her horrified eyes went from the rice container to other shelves, other boxes, other canisters. *Many* of them seemed to be moving. Many were covered with a thick layer of dark, scurrying, living creatures.

Ants.

Big, fat, black, disgusting ants.

Chapter 8

Now Maxie, her eyes slowly, slowly, circling the room, wondered how they could *not* have noticed the ants before.

What was really frightening was how *many* there were. They were everywhere, marching up and down the white walls in long, thin lines like soldiers, covering the food containers with thick coats of black, layering the white shelves with sooty streams. As Maxie and Candie looked down in horror, the fat black ants trailing across the floor in determined columns began to march up Candie's black heels and across Maxie's beige flats.

Candie shrieked and bent to swat at the invaders.

Something moved in Maxie's hair. Stomping her feet to shake the creatures from her feet, she lifted a hand to her head. Her hand came away covered with ants.

She screamed. Her head came up, her eyes darted toward the ceiling, and she screamed again. The surface overhead was covered with moving black trails.

She wanted to run, but she couldn't. Her legs seemed frozen in place.

They're just *ants*, she tried to tell herself, but it was no use. There were so *many*.

Something moved in her hair again.

Her legs thawed, and reaching down to yank Candie upright, Maxie ran for the door, dragging Candie with her.

The door was closed.

"I didn't close the door," Maxie gasped, reaching for the doorknob, "did you?"

"No! Open it, hurry!"

It was darker by the door, the light not quite reaching. Maxie, one hand shielding the top of her head, reached with her other hand for the doorknob. Her fingers closed around soft, living things, and she screamed.

"They're on the knob," she gasped, yanking the hem of her skirt upward to swat furiously at the doorknob. "They're all *over* it!"

Candie reached out a hand to help Maxie swat, and when the doorknob seemed free of crawling insects, Maxie yanked on it. Hard.

It didn't open.

"Oh, God, they're falling into my hair!" Candie cried, batting at her head with both hands. "Maxie, *get* the *door* open!"

The knob turned under Maxie's forceful grip, but the door remained stubbornly closed.

"Pound on it!" Candie shrieked, "pound!"

They both began pounding with their fists, and shouting, "Help! Open the door, *hurry*!"

Footsteps outside the pantry, then the door was pulled open, and Erica stood there, staring at them and saying, "What on earth . . . ?"

Maxie and Candie, their hands still protectively reaching for their hair, fell out into the kitchen.

Erica alerted the rest of the house to this new, latest emergency. Tinker tried to calm down Maxie and Candie, both trembling and white-faced. Then several other girls in the house, including Cath Devon, attacked the pantry with rolled-up newspapers, brooms, and cans of spray insecticide.

"I don't understand," Mildred said in a bewildered voice when the pantry was finally relatively free of pests. She leaned against the kitchen counter. "We have *never* had ants in this house. And the exterminator was just here in February, checking. There was no sign of an ant colony then. He would have said something." She sighed heavily. "I'll have to call him first thing tomorrow morning."

"There weren't any ants in there when I went in earlier," Erica said firmly. "I would have noticed."

Maxie and Candie, both still white-faced, exchanged a glance. "Tuttle was in there," Maxie said hoarsely. "Earlier. Before us."

"Tom?" the housemother said blankly. "Yes, I know. But . . . you don't think . . . ? Oh, Maxie, that's ridiculous. Why would Tom . . . ?"

Maxie shrugged. "He doesn't like us. Any of us. Haven't you noticed?"

Cath Devon, standing quietly in a corner, her face as pale as Maxie's, said hesitantly, "He's not dangerous, is he? I mean, he wouldn't really *hurt* anyone, would he?"

Maxie guessed that Cath was remembering the weird, disturbing things that had gone on when she'd lived at Nightmare Hall. She must feel right now like she'd jumped out of the frying pan into the fire.

Hastening to reassure Cath, Mildred said quickly, "No, of course not. Tom's an old crank and more than a little paranoid, I suppose, but he's never given me any reason to believe he would ever harm anyone."

Not *yet*, Maxie thought.

It seemed too much of a coincidence to her

that they'd discovered Tom Tuttle in the pantry right before they discovered the ants.

"Was anyone else in the house today who doesn't belong here?" she asked Mildred. Then she remembered. "Except for that doctor, I mean?"

Mildred looked blank. "What doctor?"

"The one whose car broke down. Big man, graying hair, handkerchief over his bloody nose? He needed to use the phone."

"Maxie, you let a stranger into the house? With everything that's been happening?" Erica demanded.

Maxie flushed. "He was a *doctor*. Had his black bag with him. He was on his way to the infirmary for a consultation. Besides, he was *hurt*. I couldn't very well just let him stand there on the front porch bleeding, could I? He was on the phone when I left. You didn't see him?"

"No, I didn't see the man," Mildred said. "That must have been when I was out back talking to Tom about the peephole and the chain lock. When I came back inside, the house was empty."

"His name was Clark," Maxie said. "Michael Clark." Desperate to be sure that she hadn't done anything foolish or dangerous, she ran to the phone and dialed the infirmary.

And was told a moment later that no Dr. Michael Clark had been expected there for a consultation or anything else.

"I don't believe it," Maxie said when she'd hung up. "I never should have let him in. It won't happen again, I promise."

"Who *was* this person?" Candie asked, a bewildered look on her face. "If he wasn't really a doctor, who *was* he and what was he doing here?"

"I don't *know* who he was," Maxie answered, "but has it crossed anyone's mind that his black bag could have been filled with . . . *ants*?"

A heavy silence followed her words.

"Mrs. B.," Maxie said shakily. "I think we need to call the police."

"No!" Erica cried. "Come on, Maxie, it was just *ants*! No one was hurt. It was a joke, a gag, a prank . . . maybe one of the other sororities did it. The police will laugh at us if we call them and tell them you were trapped in the pantry with a bunch of ants."

"Anyway," Candie reassured Maxie, "Mildred just said, Tuttle's going to put a chain lock on and a peephole in. So what happened today can't happen again, right?"

Maxie gave in reluctantly. She didn't like the idea of police officers invading Omega house any more than anyone else did. But the uneasy feeling in her stomach remained.

"What about the ceremony?" Tinker asked no one in particular. Turning to Cath, she asked, "You haven't changed your mind, have you?"

Cath laughed softly, the color returning to her face. "No, I haven't changed my mind, Tinker. Anyway," she added more soberly, "compared to what we went through at Nightmare Hall, ants are nothing."

Erica and Mildred put their heads together to figure out what to serve after the ceremony, assuming that most of the boxes in the now closed and locked pantry were ant-infested. When they had settled on ordering out for Chinese from Hunan Manor in town, preparations began again for Cath's wall-walk.

There wasn't that much to prepare. Tinker checked to make sure there was no debris lying on the top of the low brick wall. Maxie turned on the overhead lanterns strung across the lawn, while Candie and Erica sat down on the back porch and went over the routine, Cath's blindfolded walk around a low fountain wall.

Maxie was replacing a burned-out bulb in one of the lanterns when she spotted movement in the thick, tall bushes off to her left, and heard a scuttling sound. Normally, she would have dismissed the sound as a wandering cat or dog, maybe a squirrel out for a late-evening forage.

But not now.

She climbed down from her ladder and moved closer to the bushes. "Is anybody there?" she called. Candie, Cath, and Erica looked up from their bench on the porch.

"Maxie?" Erica called, standing up. "What's the matter?"

There was no answer from the bushes. Not a leaf moved, and the scuttling sound was gone.

I'm freaking, Maxie told herself, turning away. There isn't anybody there, and there never was. If I'm not careful, I'll be seeing little green men in the shadows any second now.

But she saw again the long, thick trail of ants moving across the ceiling, dropping into her hair, and began to tremble. Someone had deliberately brought those ants in from outside.

Probably in a doctor's black medical bag.

Why would someone do that?

When everything was ready, the girls gathered around the fountain under the softly glowing lanterns.

While Erica wrapped a thick, soft white cloth around Cath's eyes and tied it at the back of her head, Tinker put an audiotape into a portable cassette player. The sound that came out when she switched it on was an eerie, haunting melody played on an organ.

Horror movie music, Maxie thought to herself. Erica helped Cath up onto the low brick wall surrounding the empty concrete fountain, and the other girls formed a wide circle around the edges.

"Catherine Devon," Erica intoned in an unnaturally deep voice, "complete the circle once without faltering, and you will prove your courage and determination. This you must do for your sisters. If you succeed, we will pledge to you our eternal loyalty, as you pledge yours to us."

Cath lifted her arms straight out from her shoulders for balance and took one faltering step, then another. A light breeze ruffled her dark hair as she became more sure of her footing and began to move with confidence around the low brick wall. The music in the background filled the cool night air.

Maxie recalled her own walk, and the relief she'd felt at the end when the other sisters had removed her blindfold and hugged her, officially welcoming her to the group. Now she enjoyed the ritual again. She and Tinker on one side and Candie on the other joined hands. After dinner, she would call Brendan. Maybe they could get together that night. But she probably wouldn't tell him about the ants . . . not just yet, anyway. He'd given her a hard time about the things being stolen. Better not give him any more fuel for his argument that she should flee back to Lester.

That night, out there on the lawn under the glowing lanterns, joining hands with her sisters as they made room for a new member, she felt more at home than she ever had in the dorm.

This was the best place to be.

Until Cath fell.

Perhaps because she'd been thinking about Brendan, Maxie couldn't be sure exactly how it happened.

One minute, Cath was walking lightly, agilely, along the brick wall, and the next minute, one ankle turned sharply, she let out a soft "Ooh" and teetered slightly, her arms struggling to maintain an even balance. And then, realizing she was losing the battle, she gasped. A second later, she toppled heavily sideways.

But in the wrong direction. Had her body tipped to the right, she would have fallen onto the soft, thick grass, and been uninjured.

Instead, she fell to the left, into the fountain.

The *empty* fountain, with no cushion of water to soften the impact.

There were gasps, and then screams and shouts of horror, as Cath toppled off the wall and headed straight for the bare cement lying at the bottom of the fountain.

She tried to catch herself as she fell, and so her right arm smacked into the cement first. She screamed once, and then her head slapped against the fountain floor with a sharp crack. Cath let out a startled pained grunt before her eyes closed and she went totally limp, her right arm twisted at a strange angle beneath her.

As she lay there, as still as death, the eerie music played on.

Chapter 9

It was Erica who leaped into action first. Shouting to Candie to run and phone for an ambulance, she jumped into the fountain to see to Cath, who lay like a broken doll on the hard stone floor.

"She's alive," Erica called up to the others, who were still standing in a circle, hands over their mouths, their eyes wide with shock. "She's breathing. Someone go get a blanket."

Two more people ran to the house. One of the seniors in the group said in a voice hoarse with shock, "Nothing like this has ever happened before. How could this *happen*?"

"She fell," someone else said. "She just fell. That's all."

Maxie thought, No, she didn't. She didn't just fall. Not Cath. She's too light on her feet, too agile. And the wall isn't that narrow. We wouldn't have sent her out there if it were.

This was no simple accident. Maxie was convinced of that.

Which was why, when Cath had been taken away in a shrieking ambulance and the other girls had retreated to their rooms to talk in hushed whispers about the accident, Maxie went back outside and approached the brick wall.

Flashlight in hand, she circled the wall on her hands and knees, poking and prying at the layers of bricks with her free hand.

She found what she was looking for halfway around, at the exact spot where Cath had toppled and fallen. The bricks were all in place, so that at first glance it looked as if nothing were wrong. But when Maxie's hand reached out and poked, the top layer of bricks wobbled. When she poked further, they shifted and slid, and the layer beneath slid as well.

No wonder Cath had fallen. Her own footing had been certain, but the surface on which she was walking was unbalanced. The top two layers of brick were loose.

Maxie played the flashlight's beam across the ground beneath the wall. At its base, small clumps of dried gray mortar lay scattered randomly, like wads of discarded chewing gum.

Her eyes returned to the wall. Zeroing in on the bricks with the light, she could see faint scratch marks in the thin layer of mortar still in place. Clear evidence that someone had been digging. Tampering with the bricks. Deliberately.

Maxie sat back on her heels, a cold feeling of dread sweeping over her. Someone had known about the wall-walk. Someone had come out here and dug the mortar from between the bricks, *hoping* that Cath would fall. Without water in the fountain, there was no question that the person walking along the wall would be seriously hurt if she fell in that direction instead of onto the grass. The only question at all was which *way* she might fall, and apparently whoever had removed the mortar was willing to take that risk.

The risk had paid off. Cath Devon was lying in a hospital bed, probably with an injury to her spine.

Maxie heard again the sharp, sickening crack as Cath landed on her back in the fountain. Her stomach rose in protest. How much damage had that hard, unyielding cement done to Cath's spinal column?

They wouldn't know that until tomorrow.

Getting up slowly, as if she had suddenly aged a great deal, Maxie went back inside.

The atmosphere inside Omega house was dismal. Quiet. No music. No loud, excited chatter, normal after a wall-walk. In the dining room, the dishes Mildred had placed on the table sat empty, the candles unlit.

No one would feel like eating now.

Erica wasn't in her room. And a knock on Mildred's door brought no answer. The news about the wall being tampered with would have to wait until morning. Nothing they could do about it that night, anyway.

When Maxie returned to her own room, she told Tinker what she had discovered.

Tinker wasn't surprised. "It seems to me," she said solemnly when Maxie had changed into the oversized T-shirt she slept in and sat down on her bed, "that the only person who would want to ruin the ceremony would be someone who was mad that they weren't taking *part* in it."

"You mean like Isabella or Holly?" Brendan had suggested the same thing. Had Erica ever checked the list? She hadn't said anything about talking to either of the girls. Maybe she hadn't had time.

Tinker nodded. "Exactly. I just can't think of anyone else who would want to hurt Cath. Who would hate someone as nice and as quiet as Cath? She's not the kind of person to have enemies." Tinker's eyes were clouded with shock and fatigue. "I don't want to think about this anymore. It's too depressing. I'm going to sleep."

But as Tinker's breath deepened, evened out and became the steady breathing of a deep sleeper, Maxie wondered if that really *was* the right answer. And then an even creepier thought forced its way into her mind.

After what had happened to Cath, it might be stupid to pass off the events of the past few days as simple game-playing. It could be something much worse. Maybe the person responsible *wasn't* just playing games.

Maybe he or she was . . . crazy. Over the edge. A loose cannon. It might have all *started* as a game, but now . . .

Crazy?

How could a crazy person be running around Omega house without anyone noticing?

When she finally climbed into bed in the darkened room, it struck her that in all the time she'd been in Omega house, she had never heard it so completely silent. It wasn't just that everyone was asleep. Maxie often pulled all-nighters to get a paper written, so she knew the silence of the sleeping house.

But on this night, the silence was different.

Now the air seemed still as if everyone in the house were holding her breath. Waiting in fear for whatever would happen next.

Chapter 10

Maxie dressed quickly the next morning, intent on giving Erica the bad news about the brick wall.

But when she went to Erica's room and knocked, there was no answer. Probably taking a shower.

Maxie wasn't willing to wait. Mildred would have to be told first. The police had to be notified. Even if she was wrong about the wall, and she was positive that she wasn't, the police would have scientific ways of proving whether or not the wall had actually been tampered with. Then they'd find the person who had done it and take him or her away, so that life at Omega house could return to normal.

Maxie found Mildred in the kitchen. When the news about the wall had registered, Mildred promptly went to the wall telephone to call the Twin Falls police.

Erica, fresh from a shower, her long, blonde hair still damp, was on the telephone when Maxie went upstairs. Tinker was in the room, too. She signaled to Maxie to come in and take a seat while Erica finished her conversation.

When Erica hung up, she sagged against the wall and said with enormous relief, "That was the hospital. Cath's going to be okay. No permanent damage to the spine."

"Oh, that's great!" Maxie felt sorry for Erica. She had ridden to the hospital in the ambulance with Cath last night, but because she wasn't a relative, hadn't been allowed to see the patient, and had finally left without knowing Cath's condition. The strain had left her oval face very pale. She probably hadn't slept much.

"Her arm is broken, though," Erica continued, "and she has a concussion. She'll be in the hospital for a few days. Mildred already called her parents."

"Mildred told me the only time something like this happened before was when your mom was hurt in a hazing incident," Tinker said. "They did it differently, then . . . nothing as tame as a wall-walk. She said something about the railroad bridge behind campus?"

Erica nodded. "Yeah, she had to walk it. She fell into the river. She was in a full body cast for eight weeks and didn't graduate with her class. Had to finish up in summer school. Her accident was responsible for some new rules about hazing."

"I'm sure the university will launch an investigation into Cath's accident," Tinker said, just as grimly.

"Maybe that's what someone wanted," Maxie commented, and filled Erica and Tinker in on what she'd found at the wall. "Anyone who knew about the wall-walking and tampered with those bricks had to know that if Cath got hurt, the administration would hear about it and we'd be in hot water. And Cath *did* get hurt."

"Why would someone *do* that?" Erica asked, a puzzled frown on her face.

Glancing at Tinker, Maxie said, "Tinker thinks it could have been someone we rejected. Brendan does, too. Did you ever check that list or talk to any of the girls we rushed but didn't pledge?"

Erica shook her head. "I haven't had time." She flushed guiltily. "Maybe if I had, Cath wouldn't be in the hospital now."

"It's not your fault. Those bricks could have been tampered with before we even thought of the list, so quit blaming yourself. Anyway,

Mildred's calling the police. They'll find out what really happened."

Erica's face blanched at the word "police."

Mildred came up to tell them the police would be going to the hospital first, to see if Cath was able to tell them anything, and would then come out to Omega house to check the wall. "It won't be until after classes, so go ahead and do what you usually do."

The first person Maxie ran into on campus was Brendan. She could tell by the set of his mouth that he'd already heard about Cath.

"Must have been pretty bad," he said as they met on the steps of the administration buiding, Butler Hall, "if they took her to the hospital instead of the infirmary."

"We thought it was worse than it really was," Maxie said defensively. A sharp, chilling March wind had arisen, and Maxie shivered in her red ski jacket. "She landed on her back, and we thought maybe . . . but she just has a concussion and a broken arm."

Brendan's dark eyebrows tilted. "Just?"

Maxie flushed. "I didn't mean 'just.' I meant, that's a lot better than a spinal cord injury, right?"

He sat down on the top step, off to one side, and yanked at her wrist to get her to join him.

She sat reluctantly. She didn't want to have

this conversation. But if they didn't talk about it, it would get in their way. What had happened to Cath would stand between them like a brick wall. Brick wall . . . Maxie saw Cath falling again, her arms flailing out around her, and felt sick.

"I hear you're in trouble with the administration," Brendan said.

Maxie nodded. "We all have to see the Dean and explain what happened. I'm on my way there now."

"What *did* happen?"

She told him.

Brendan's head swiveled in shock as Maxie explained about the loose bricks.

"On purpose?" he shouted. "You're saying someone did this on purpose?"

She shrugged. "Looks that way. Mildred talked to the police, and we have to talk to them this afternoon."

"So," he said, looking directly at her, "when are you packing?"

Hadn't she known this was coming? "I'm not, Brendan. I'm not a rat who deserts a sinking ship."

"Oh, it's sinking, all right." Brendan's strongly angled face reddened with anger. "And you've decided to go down with it? You're not its captain, Maxie. Let Erica go down with the ship, but you get *out* of there!"

She tried to tell herself it was because he cared about her. She tried to tell herself that if he *didn't* care about her, it wouldn't make any difference to him whether she left the house or not.

But it didn't help. She needed his support now, his help, not his direct order that she leave the house and her sisters when they were in trouble. Angry, she retorted, "Would you want me to desert *you* if you were in trouble? I'm not leaving the house, Brendan. And if all you can do is tell me that that's the answer, I don't want to talk about this anymore." Jumping up, she turned and ran into the building.

The Dean listened to her story, said she would talk to Mildred about increased security at Omega house, and then delivered a mild lecture on the university's rules against any kind of hazing. Then Maxie was excused.

She was halfway to her ten o'clock class when a tall, heavyset girl with frizzy dark hair approached her. Isabella Sands, one of the girls Omega Phi had rejected.

The little hairs on the back of Maxie's neck stood on end. Not *now*, she thought, and then quickly thought better of it. Erica hadn't had time to talk to Isabella or Holly. No time like the present, she decided.

Isabella matched her steps to Maxie's. "I heard about Cath," she said with a mournful tone to her voice that Maxie immediately tagged as phony. "But I guess she's going to be okay, hmm?"

Maxie nodded.

"But," eagerness crept into Isabella's voice, "she won't be finishing out the year at Omega house, right? I mean, she'll probably be in the hospital for a while, and then maybe she'll have to go home to recuperate, don't you think?"

Maxie was tired, her argument with Brendan and her nerve-wracking interview in the Dean's office had tied her nerves in knots, and the gray, chilly day was no comfort. She stopped walking, turned to Isabella and said, "Isabella. You weren't rejected by Omega Phi because there wasn't any *room* for you. You were rejected because you are the sort of person who follows people around campus trying to take advantage of the fact that a very nice girl has been hurt in an accident. Omega Phis aren't like that. And we don't want anyone who *is*." Having said that, Maxie turned and walked away, leaving Isabella standing in the center of the commons, her jaw descending toward her neck.

I probably shouldn't have done that, Maxie told herself as she hurried to class. I didn't learn a single thing about Isabella except that she's a creep, and if she was already mad at us, I probably just made her even madder. Then a tiny smile slid across her face. But it felt *so* good!

Later in the morning, Maxie was approached by Holly Dukes, also with an eye toward taking Cath's place at Omega house. But this time, she dispatched the Omega wannabe even more swiftly than she had Isabella.

Vultures! she thought angrily, stomping away from Holly. We were right to vote against both of them.

But just how far would either of the girls go to get into the house, Maxie wondered. Head down against the wind, she made her way to the student center to meet Candie for lunch. Was there violence in Isabella or Holly? Isabella's dark eyes had a flat, cruel look to them. Holly might *seem* shy, but hadn't she, too, tracked Maxie down on campus to see about her chances of taking Cath's place? Her determination seemed to be overcoming her shyness. How determined *was* she? And what could that determination drive her to do?

A few feet away from the entrance to the student center, Maxie saw Candie standing under a huge old tree, the wind blowing her reddish-brown hair around her face. But she wasn't alone. She was with someone, and she was arguing.

Peering more closely at the pair from a distance, Maxie recognized the tall, broad-shouldered guy Candie was arguing with. Graham Lucas, the very person who had been pestering Candie with notes and flowers and phone calls.

Why was Candie even *talking* to him? A feeling of dread swept over Maxie. They had all agreed, when Candie told them what was going on, that the best tactic was to ignore Graham, thinking that eventually he'd give up and go away.

Except, he hadn't. Candie had told Graham about Dylan, but he didn't seem to care that she already had a boyfriend. Candie said he was still phoning repeatedly and sending her little notes.

What Maxie didn't understand was why Graham hadn't given up. Candie was beautiful and fun and smart, but so were other girls on campus. His refusal to take the hint — even the insults — of Candie, and keep hanging on, wasn't . . . *normal*.

Maxie hurried over to them. "C'mon, Candie," she urged, barely glancing at Graham, "let's go!"

As they hurried away, Maxie glanced over her shoulder. Graham was staring after them, his eyes narrowed, his face scarlet with rage.

"Whoa!" she said to Candie, "stay *away* from that guy, okay? He looks like he's about to pop a few blood vessels. Why were you even talking to him?"

"I was just about to go into the center when I heard someone calling me. When I saw that it was him, I was going to keep going, but he yelled that he had some news about Cath, so I walked over to see what it was. And of *course* he didn't know a thing about Cath. He just wanted to know why I hadn't been taking his phone calls." Candie laughed softly. "I told him it was because talking to him on the phone was worse than going to the dentist."

"Candie! You shouldn't antagonize him. He looked so furious back there."

Candie shrugged and pulled open the door to the student center. "You *have* to be rude to guys like that. It's the only thing they understand. If you're nice, they're harder to get rid of than fungus."

Maybe, Maxie thought as they joined Jenna, waiting at a table by the window in the small, cozy cafe. But Candie had *been* rude to Graham. More than once. So why hadn't he disappeared?

Late that afternoon, when only a naive new sister named Chloe Bannister was in the house, the doorbell rang.

Chloe opened the front door to see a young man in a white uniform, armed with a red canister, standing on the front porch.

"Can I help you?" she asked.

Thick red hair showed under his white cap as he adjusted his sunglasses. "Yes, ma'am. Actually, I'm here to help *you*. I'm with ZAPCO Exterminators. You were expecting me, right?"

"Oh, yes." Chloe opened the door wider, then remembered the procedure they'd been warned to follow. "Could I see your identification, please?" she asked politely.

"Sure. No problem." The young man reached into a back pocket and pulled out a vinyl card case, flipped it open and held it out.

Chloe read it carefully. Nodded. "I guess it's okay. If you need anything, I'll be in the living room."

"Thank you," the exterminator said and, whistling a cheerful tune, began marching through the house.

Chapter 11

When Maxie got home, Erica was in her room, studying. She had already called the hospital to see how Cath was doing. "She's awake and feeling better, but she'll probably be there another four or five days."

Her tone of voice was so despondent, Maxie felt compelled to say, "It wasn't your fault, Erica. Someone tampered with the bricks. Have the police been here yet?"

"No. They're coming after dinner. We're all supposed to be here. They'll want to talk to everyone." Erica sighed heavily. "Not that we have any answers." Then, "Did you see the new peephole?"

"What new peephole?"

"On the front door. Tuttle put it in, so we can see who's out on the porch before we open the door. And he put a new chain lock on the door, too. But," Erica's mouth turned downward, "that's all the university would spring for right now. According to Mildred, the Dean said there wasn't any real evidence of a pressing need for more security." Her grimace deepened. "I guess he means, there aren't any dead bodies lying around the house."

Not *yet*, Maxie thought involuntarily, and quickly banished the thought from her mind. "Maybe the Dean will change her mind after the police tell her the wall around the fountain was deliberately tampered with."

"Don't hold your breath. She might just point out that the wall is *outside*, so what good would installing a security system *inside* the house do?"

Tired of the whole subject, Maxie asked, "Brendan hasn't called, has he?"

"No. Was he supposed to?"

"I guess not," Maxie answered vaguely, and thought, Liar! He was *definitely* supposed to call. To deliver an apology for not being more supportive. If you couldn't turn to your boyfriend when things were going wrong, who could you turn to?

Dinner was a gloomy affair. There seemed to Maxie to be two groups of people at the table: those who ate for comfort because they were uneasy about the upcoming visit by the police, and those who couldn't eat at all, for exactly the same reason. Maxie was in the latter group. She barely touched her food.

As she and Tinker began carrying plates to the kitchen, Tinker muttered, "I wish they'd hurry up and get here. The sooner we get this over with, the faster things will return to normal in this house. We're all walking around like this place is full of land mines."

"Because that's the way it *feels*," Maxie agreed.

"Well, I think it's getting to me," Tinker said, dropping her stack of plates on the kitchen counter. "I don't feel so hot." Her hands went to her stomach. "Can you finish here? I — " she turned suddenly and ran from the room. Maxie heard her feet pounding up the stairs.

Tinker, sick? Tinker was never sick.

Before Maxie could go after Tinker to check on her, the doorbell rang. Maxie hurried out to answer it. Using the peephole felt strange, as if she were studying someone under a microscope. Two uniformed police officers, a man and a woman, were waiting on the front porch. The woman held up a gold badge. As far as Maxie could tell, it was an authentic police badge, so she let them in.

She closed the door when they were inside, turned around, and came face-to-face with Erica, who had come to greet the two officers.

But the sorority's president couldn't even manage a "hello." She was clearly ill. She looked terrible. Her face was contorted in pain and had a greenish pallor to it. A fine sheen of sweat covered her skin, and her hands were placed protectively over her stomach.

"Erica?" Maxie said, moving toward her, "what's wrong?" But before she reached the spot where Erica stood with her face twisted in agony, Erica's knees buckled, and she crumpled to the floor, writhing in pain.

As the officers moved to Erica's side, Tinker and Candie came into the foyer, both walking unsteadily, their faces the same color as Erica's. Tinker held one hand to her mouth, the other pressed against her stomach. Candie leaned heavily on the railing as they struggled up the stairs. The sound of a door closing on the second floor was followed by painful retching sounds.

The kitchen door opened as Mildred emerged to clear the rest of the dishes from the dining room. When she saw Erica lying on her back, her knees drawn up against what was obviously severe pain, she rushed to kneel beside the fallen girl. "What's happening?" she cried. "Maxie, what is *wrong* with Erica?"

Before Maxie could answer honestly that she

didn't know, two more girls came staggering out of the kitchen, groaning.

Mildred took one look at them and said urgently to the police officers, "You'd better get an ambulance over here. Something is terribly wrong."

One of the officers went outside to make the call. The other stayed behind, taking Erica's pulse, asking Maxie to go get a glass of water.

When she returned, Mildred lifted her head to ask, "Maxie, what *is* this? What's happened? Erica looks like she's . . . like she's *dying*!"

"So do the others," Maxie agreed. "Tinker and Candie, and Morgan and Sarah." A trio of girls made their way out of the kitchen and into the living room, where they flopped on a pair of leather couches. "And Sheila and Dennie and Nita don't look so hot, either."

"But . . . but *you're* not sick, Maxie?" Mildred asked with concern.

Erica groaned. She seemed to be having trouble breathing, and she drew her knees up even closer to her stomach.

"No. I'm not. But . . ." Maxie was too confused to think straight, but one solid thought slipped into her mind . . . "but I didn't eat anything at dinner. Everyone who's sick *did*. I remember Nita and Dennie especially saying how good it tasted, and Erica and Candie taking second helpings."

"Dinner?" Mildred paled. "The spaghetti?"

Maxie nodded.

"Well, it couldn't have been that," Mildred said. "I made it myself. The meat was fresh, and so was the sauce. There couldn't have been anything wrong with it."

"Any of it left?" the policeman asked.

"Yes. I put the leftovers in the frig." Mildred led him out into the kitchen. Maxie followed them to wet a cloth for Erica's forehead.

The officer took the plastic-covered bowl off its shelf. He lifted the plastic wrap and sniffed.

"Any objection if I take this with me, ma'am?" the officer asked, holding up the bowl.

"Oh, heavens," Mildred murmured, "if there's anything wrong with something I cooked, if that's what made my girls sick, I . . ."

"It probably isn't, Mrs. B.," Maxie said hastily. "But he should check it anyway, right? Just to prove that it *wasn't* the spaghetti. It's probably just a flu bug or something, really." But as she went upstairs to check on Tinker and Candie, she knew she hadn't meant a word of it. She didn't really believe it was a bug. What kind of "bug" would hit so many people at exactly the same moment, or do so much damage?

Tinker and Candie were in bad shape.

It seemed to Maxie that it was hours before the ambulance came shrieking up the driveway. And even more hours before a doctor came into the emergency waiting room at the hospital to tell Mildred and the girls who hadn't eaten dinner that they had stabilized all of the patients.

"Looks like botulism," he told a hand-wringing Mildred. "They must have eaten something that was spoiled. Home-canned, maybe?"

"No, no," Mildred said frantically, "that's not possible! That meat was fresh, the sauce was fresh . . . it couldn't be botulism!"

"What's botulism?" a girl named Nancy, who hadn't eaten, asked.

"Comes from home-canned foods that go bad, usually," the doctor said matter-of-factly. "You didn't can the tomatoes yourself?" he asked Mildred.

"No. The tomatoes were fresh."

"Didn't let the meat thaw on the counter?"

Ashen-faced, Mildred answered firmly, "No. I always thaw meat in the refrigerator. I know what I'm *doing* in the kitchen, doctor."

The doctor nodded absentmindedly, seemingly unaware of Mildred's anxious state of mind. Telling them he was keeping everyone overnight, adding that they should know by the following day what had made the girls sick, he left, a puzzled frown on his face.

The two police officers, who had accompanied them to the hospital, approached the worried group.

"Couldn't help overhearing," the male officer said. "If it isn't what that doctor said he thought it was, botulism, any idea what it might be?"

They all shook their heads no.

"Had to be in the food," the female officer said. "The ones who ate dinner got sick, the ones who didn't are okay. Doesn't take a genius to figure out that it was the food, all right. But," she added kindly, addressing her comment to Mildred, "that doesn't mean it was something you did wrong. Could be someone added to your seasoning, if you get my meaning."

Mildred looked at her as if she had just stepped out of a spaceship. "Excuse me?"

Maxie held her breath. She wasn't going to like what the officer was going to say, she could feel it.

"Well, ma'am, we came to your house in the first place tonight because someone landed in the hospital, right? We haven't had a chance to check things out yet. But if it wasn't an accident . . . well, all I'm getting at is, if someone sent *that* girl to the hospital, maybe someone sent these other girls to the hospital, too. Anyone in your house today with access to that spaghetti?"

Maxie's stomach rolled over.

Mildred wasn't happy about it, either. "I . . . just the girls," she said weakly. Then she added, "Oh, well an exterminator came but . . ."

The female police officer looked interested. "Exterminator, ma'am?"

"Yes. We had a . . . a slight ant problem. I called ZAPCO, the company I use regularly, and they sent a young man out today. I wasn't home at the time, but Chloe let him in, didn't you, Chloe? What did you say his name was, dear? A Mr. Dillon?"

"Dooley," Cleo said. "Real young. Kind of cute, too. He had real bright red, curly hair. Like I said, cute. Seemed to know what he was doing. I mean, he had a tank of chemicals and a uniform and everything. And I checked his identification," she added nervously. "He had a business card with his name on it."

The officer pulled a small white notebook from her chest pocket. "Company van, miss? You check that out, too?"

Chloe's round face flushed. "Yes, absolutely. ZAPCO. That was the name."

"Officer," Mildred interjected, "I've used this company before. I just told you that. They wouldn't send someone who would be sloppy enough to contaminate our food with those nasty chemicals, if that's what you're implying."

Making no comment, the officer turned to her partner and said in a low voice, "Have the lab check for insecticide. Make the call *now*."

Maxie heard her clearly. Insecticide? She thought Erica and Tinker and the others had ingested bug-killer? *Bug*-killer?

If it killed bugs, what did it do to people?

The doctor hadn't said they'd all be okay. He'd only said they were "stabilized," whatever that meant. That they weren't at death's door, Maxie guessed. Not much comfort there.

It was all too much. The house that she loved had become a place where people ingested deadly chemicals? And the police thought someone had deliberately made that happen?

The officer who had gone to the phone turned around. "Had to roust the manager at home," he told them. "ZAPCO doesn't have a Mr. Dooley working for them, never did. And one of their trucks was stolen last night, returned after work hours tonight. That van had loaded canisters in the back, and the manager says it probably even had an extra uniform or two."

Maxie's knees turned to mush and she slid into a red plastic chair.

For the first time since she had moved into Omega house, she was afraid to go home.

Chapter 12

Maxie decided to spend the night at Lester with Jenna. She knew she couldn't face returning to Omega house while Tinker and Candie were still in the hospital.

Jenna was thrilled to see her. She raced around the room, grabbing clean sheets and making up the empty bed, chattering a mile a minute the whole time.

"Grotesque!" she declared when Maxie explained why she was there. "I mean, as thrilled as I am to see your gorgeous self, I wasn't sitting around wishing illness upon your sorority sisters. So, they're going to recover and spring from their hospital beds whole and healthy again, right?"

Maxie didn't know. "I hope so." She sat down on the newly made bed. "The police hinted that maybe someone had put something in our food."

Jenna, on the other bed, stared at her. "You mean on purpose? Like, deliberately? As in poisoning the wine in some cheap detective novel?" •

"Um-hmm. They're back at Omega house now, checking the brick wall around the fountain. They'll see what I saw . . . that the bricks have been tampered with. I guess once they see that, they'll really be sure that someone poisoned the spaghetti."

"Maxie," Jenna said, leaning forward, dyed bangs falling carelessly across her forehead, "*what* is going on over there?"

"I don't know. The only person in the house yesterday who didn't belong there was an exterminator. But Chloe said he had I.D."

"Oh, Maxie, getting fake I.D. is as easy as writing a check. Anyone can get fake I.D. And uniforms and anything else they need. My dad says people do it all the time." Jenna's father was a policeman in Albany. "Freaks him out, how easy it is to pretend to be someone you're not."

"Well, what are we supposed to *do*?" Maxie cried, tears of frustration spilling over. "If Mrs. B. calls people to come to the house and then someone shows up with identification, how are we supposed to know they're fake?"

"Well, that's what freaks my dad," Jenna

answered calmly. "Listen, just be grateful you had no appetite tonight, right? But if you didn't partake, you must be starved now. What say we hit Vinnie's, or the diner? Might be just the thing to make you feel human again."

Maxie didn't feel like eating. But the eager look on Jenna's face stopped her from saying so. It wouldn't kill her, she decided, to act like she was happy to be here with Jenna. The truth was, she felt uncomfortable in this room now, probably because she felt guilty about leaving Omega house at such a terrible time. But Jenna didn't need to know that.

"Let me just splash some water on my face and brush my hair," Maxie said.

In the bathroom, she stared at her face in the mirror as if she didn't recognize it. Her hair was a tangled mess, her eyes red-rimmed, her skin pasty. I might not be sick like the others, she thought with disgust, but I *look* like I am.

She couldn't find a washcloth. Bending to open the door to the cupboard under the sink, she rummaged around until she found one. She was about to straighten up when something caught her eye. Something bright red, fluffy. There hadn't been anything bright red and fluffy under there when she lived in room 316. What *was* it?

She reached in and lifted it out. Held it in

her hands. Turned it over several times, examining it.

A wig.

A bright red, curly wig.

Chloe's words rang in her ears. "He had this really bright red, curly hair. Cute, like I said."

"What are you doing?" Jenna said from the doorway. "Where did you get that?"

Maxie lifted her head. "In the cupboard. I was looking for a washcloth. What is it?" She stood up, the wig still in her hands. "I mean, I *know* what it is. But what's it for?"

Jenna reached out and took the wig from her. "Don't you remember? Halloween. I was Little Orphan Annie. I wore this to the party at the student center." She opened the cupboard door and tossed the wig back inside. "Oh, that's right," she said as she straightened up, "you weren't there. You went to a sorority thing that night. So you never saw my costume." She shrugged. "Too bad. I looked pretty cute."

"I invited you to Omega's party," Maxie said a bit defensively, feeling as if she'd been accused of something. "You wouldn't come."

"Didn't belong there," Jenna said briskly, and then quickly smiled. "Look, I had fun where I was, okay?" She turned away. "Come on, hurry up. I'm ravenous."

Maxie was too unsettled to hurry. Something Brendan had said was nagging at her. Brendan had suggested that the person tormenting the Omega Phis might be a reject. He'd meant someone not pledged by the sorority. But there were *other* kinds of rejection, weren't there? Like . . . like rejection of a former roommate and best friend. Maxie had once seen Jenna dump everything off her desk and throw a hairbrush across the room because she was angry at the guy she was seeing at the time. There had been fury in her round, usually placid face. Pure, unrestrained fury. Her eyes had blazed, the pupils narowing into tiny pinpoints.

When she'd calmed down enough to notice Maxie staring at her, Jenna had laughed self-consciously and said, "Forgot to tell you, I've got my dad's temper. Don't look so scared. I only attack things, not people."

Was that still true?

The question shocked Maxie. What am I *thinking*? she wondered, feeling sick to her stomach. Jenna? What's wrong with me? I'm coming unglued here.

Anyway, the doctor, the exterminator — those had been *guys* who had come to Omega house. Not a blonde *girl*.

Not Jenna. Definitely not Jenna.

Get a grip, Maxie, she told herself, and left the bathroom.

Although it was nearly midnight on a weeknight, the long silver diner was packed. Some students were using Burgers Etc. as an escape from hours of studying, while others had stopped in on their way home from a movie in town.

Brendan was standing by the jukebox, talking to a tall girl with long, blonde hair.

She looks like Erica from the back, Maxie thought, her stab of jealousy defeated by her concern for the hospitalized Erica.

When Brendan turned around, laughing, and saw Maxie and Jenna heading for a booth, he hesitated, and then walked toward them. Alone.

He wasn't *with* that girl, whoever she was. Maxie smiled at him, forgetting for the moment that he hadn't called to apologize after their argument, hadn't come to Omega house to talk to her. He didn't even know yet that many of her sorority sisters were in the hospital. She dreaded telling him. He'd have a fit.

To her surprise, he didn't. His reaction when she'd told him after they gave the waitress their order was one of concern, not anger. "You think they're all going to be okay?" he asked.

Too surprised to speak, Maxie only nodded.

He'd been so anxious for her to leave Omega house when the other things had happened. Why not now? Maybe he was as sick of the arguing as she was. "I guess so. We won't know for sure until tomorrow, when they tell us what was in the spaghetti sauce. The doctor thinks it's some kind of chemical."

"Chemical?"

"Tell him the whole story, Maxie," Jenna urged.

Well, he hadn't exploded yet. She might as well tell the whole truth and nothing but. And so she told him all about the fake exterminator and the spaghetti sauce.

"But . . . you're not sick," Brendan said.

"I didn't eat. Some of us didn't, and we're still fine. That's why the police are convinced it was the spaghetti."

"They think someone sprayed chemicals on your food? You mean, like insecticide?"

"Well, actually, it could have been anything. Since the guy wasn't really *from* ZAPCO, he could have had something else in the tank. Some kind of plain old poison, maybe. Erica looked *so* sick. . . . I was afraid she was dying."

Their food came then, ending the conversation. But Maxie was unable to take even one bite from her hamburger. She kept seeing the faces of her friends, twisted in pain.

She tried to push the ugly picture out of her head. All around her, people were eating and talking and laughing and playing the jukebox. The diner was a warm, friendly place to be, and she was perfectly safe here. Why couldn't she relax like the others?

Because I'm *scared*, came the answer, and they're not.

"I have to get out of here," she said suddenly, standing up.

"I'll drive you back to Omega house," Brendan said, sliding out of the booth.

"Oh, she's not staying there tonight," Jenna said quickly, jumping up, wiping her mouth with a napkin. "She's staying with me."

Oh, boy, Maxie thought, her stomach churning. "Jenna, I can't," she said earnestly, "I just can't. I know I said I would, and I wanted to, but I've got to go back to Omega house. I just don't feel right about not being there when so much is going on."

Jenna's round face fell. "You can't possibly want to go back there when you're so much safer at Lester with me."

Maxie stood her ground. "I have to go. Please understand, Jenna. Please?"

Jenna sagged against the booth and her mouth twisted. "Sure, I understand," she said heavily. "I guess I just can't compete with all your 'sisters.' "

"Jenna . . ." But it was too late. Jenna had already turned away.

Maxie watched her saunter, oh so casually, over to another booth. "I hurt her feelings," she told Brendan, her voice heavy with regret. "But I really do need to get back to the house."

"She'll survive. C'mon, let's go." He paid the bill, and they left.

She wanted to stay in Brendan's car forever. She felt safe there, sitting amid all the clutter and the smells of after-shave and peppermint breath-savers and the riper smell of gym clothes. They would just ride forever, up and down the highway, where nothing at Omega house could touch them.

But that wasn't possible.

She was at least grateful to Brendan for not insisting again that she move out of the house.

"Thanks," she said as he walked her up the wide stone steps to the front porch. "Not just for the ride. For not arguing with me about leaving here, especially after I told you what happened here tonight."

"Forget it. I know when I'm licked. You made that clear when you stomped away from me at Butler Hall. I had no business telling you what to do, anyway."

"This is true," she said lightly, turning at the front door to face him. "But I guess I don't blame you for trying." She raised her arms to encircle his neck. "I know you were just worried about me."

"Still am. More now than before." He put his hands on her shoulders, drew her close. "The truth is, though," he murmured into her ear, "if you only did what I told you to, this relationship would be about as exciting as a pair of old shoes. Easier, maybe," he added with a rueful laugh, "but not much fun, right?"

"Right," Maxie agreed, laughing.

He was about to kiss her for a second time when a deep voice from the foot of the steps said, "Well, now, I thought there wasn't to be no congregatin' on the front porch." A snicker followed the comment.

Maxie pulled abruptly away from Brendan. "Tuttle! What are you doing out here?"

"Heard there was some trouble over here. Heard it on the radio. Bunch of girls carted off to the hospital, man on the radio says. So I come to see what it's all about. Sounded like you girls been eatin' somethin' you shouldn't of."

Maxie was sure she heard a sly grin in that voice, lost in the shadows at the foot of the steps. "Everyone's in bed," she said sharply.

"Everyone 'cept you. *You* could fill me in."

"Not now, Tuttle. Come back in the morning."

He put one foot on the bottom step. "I don't think it'd be right of me to leave till I know you're safe and sound inside. I gotta watch out for you girls."

Creep! Everyone knew he did most of his "watching" through the windows! But it was obvious that he was going to stay right there at the foot of the steps until Brendan left.

Telling Brendan she'd see him tomorrow, and giving him a gentle shove, Maxie turned and went into the house.

Maxie slid the new chain lock into place, pulled the curtain aside to make certain that Tuttle had disappeared, and when she was sure that he had, she went upstairs to bed.

Chapter 13

The police returned to Omega house the following day with disturbing news. There had been no trace of insecticide or any other kind of poison in the spaghetti taken from the house. They would like, they said, to be given some of the dishes used in serving the food.

Too late. The plates and the silverware had all gone through the dishwasher, which rendered them useless to the police.

To further complicate matters, the doctor at the hospital had changed his initial diagnosis. The girls were recovering too quickly, he said, for botulism. Probably simple food poisoning, although it couldn't have been the spaghetti, then. Wouldn't have worked on them that fast. Had to have been something they ate for lunch, instead.

Mildred's relief at this news was visible. None of the girls had eaten lunch at Omega house. She was blameless, after all.

But the girls affected had not all eaten lunch at the same place, which further confused the police. Different restaurants, cafes, and dining halls were involved, yet apparently only the girls from Omega house had fallen victim.

"Wish we had those plates," one officer said regretfully as they turned to leave the sorority house. "Can't be sure of anything now."

They were no more confused than Maxie. She had been so sure that the phony exterminator had done something to the spaghetti. If not, what was he doing in the house?

The worst consequence was that now the university definitely wouldn't spring for more security.

The police did agree with her that the bricks in the fountain wall had been tampered with. But they didn't seem to be taking it nearly as seriously as she did. They seemed to regard it as a "prank" gone bad. Shaking their heads and making comments about the stupidity of initiation rituals, the police officers left, telling the housemother to call them if anything else came up.

Maxie left for class thoroughly dispirited. Although her ill sorority sisters would be coming home that afternoon, the help that she had hoped for hadn't arrived, after all. No one, not even the police, knew what was going on. They didn't even seem to believe that anything *was* going on.

But she was sure. Positive. The loosened bricks hadn't been a prank, and neither had the stolen things so mysteriously returned, or the disgusting ants in the pantry. And whatever it was that had sent her sisters to the hospital, it had to have come from the phony exterminator. Nothing else made sense.

Oh, who am I kidding? she thought as she hurried along campus, too preoccupied to notice the tiniest of buds sprouting on the crab apple trees or the tips of snow crocuses pushing their heads up through the cold, hard ground. *None* of this makes sense!

It was almost April. But to Maxie, the day seemed like the darkest day of the winter.

Her sisters came home, pale and drained, and went promptly to bed. Maxie did what she could to make them more comfortable.

Jenna called. "I heard your compadres were sprung. Must be a really cheery atmosphere over there right about now. Feel like coming over here to escape your cares and woes?"

Annoyed, Maxie said sharply, "Jenna, I can't leave now! I'm going to help Mildred give everyone soup later on."

An offended silence met her ears. Then,

"Right. And since I don't have two good hands, I couldn't possibly be asked to help." Click. Jenna had hung up.

It took Maxie a few stunned minutes to recover. What was Jenna talking about? Of course she had two good hands. But . . .

Then she got it. Jenna had wanted to be asked to help at Omega house. And why not? She was not only a friend of Maxie's, she knew many of the girls in the sorority. They would probably have been grateful if she'd shown up.

And why hadn't she been asked?

Maxie dialed Jenna's number so fast her fingers dialed a two instead of a three and she got a wrong number. Concentrating, she dialed again.

No answer.

Jenna had probably left the room in a fury. Who could blame her? Of all the snobbish, callous . . .

Maxie couldn't stand herself.

But she was soon so busy she had to put Jenna's hurt feelings out of her mind.

Soup, toast, and tea did a lot to restore the spirits of the ailing girls. A few came downstairs to watch television later that night, and by the next morning, all but three attempted to go to classes. Several of that group came home early, however, and decided to take the rest of the week off.

"Food poisoning stinks," a girl named Sam declared emphatically as she struggled up the stairs. "I'm going back to bed. Don't wake me up until Sunday morning."

"There's a party at Tri-Delt Saturday night," Maxie reminded her.

Sam visibly brightened. "Okay, then, Saturday afternoon. Not a minute sooner."

Maxie tried to tell herself that with the police on the alert, with the peephole in the front door and the new chain lock installed, and with warnings to check all identification carefully before letting anyone in, Omega house was as safe as any other house on campus.

And as her friends recovered and laughter and chatter and music again began to take their rightful place in the house, she felt some of her tension easing away.

The rest of the week passed without event. Candie was still fielding calls from Graham Lucas. Jenna was cool when she spoke to Maxie on campus and Maxie was at a loss as to how to apologize for her thoughtlessness. But everything else seemed normal. There were no new visitors to the house, no more insects in the pantry, and no one caught Tom Tuttle staring in the windows.

By Saturday afternoon, the fully recovered patients decided to head out to the mall. Everyone went but Maxie. The thought of having the house all to herself was just too tempting. A few days earlier, the thought would have set her teeth on edge. Now, she felt grateful for the solitude. It was a bright, sunny afternoon and nothing bad had happened since the spaghetti incident. She decided to start off with a long, hot shower.

Her hair was still wet, hanging loosely down her back, when the telephone shrilled.

It was Brendan. "You're going to hate me," he said cautiously. "I can't make the Tri-Delt party tonight."

"Oh, Brendan. Why not?"

"Gotta do a friend a big favor. Charlie Donovan's sister went and got herself engaged. Big-deal engagement party tonight over in Charlie's hometown, Shadrach. About eighty miles over the hill. He doesn't have wheels and he's desperate for a ride. I said I'd take him."

"Brendan!" Was she whining? She hated whiners. So did Brendan. "Why can't he take a bus?"

"Shadrach is a town of three thousand people, Maxie. They have a gas station, a grocery store, and a dairy. They do not have a bus station. Therefore, buses do not go there."

"Oh, Brendan." She wouldn't whine anymore. "I was counting on having a little time with you. . . . Is there any chance you'll be back in time to catch the last few minutes?"

"No can do. I'm staying to bring him back home. Ninety minutes to get there, a couple of hours at the sister's party, and then ninety minutes back here. It'll be late. Maybe we'll catch a movie tomorrow night, okay?"

Giving up, Maxie told him it was okay, to drive safely, and to call her tomorrow. Then she slowly, regretfully replaced the receiver.

It wouldn't be as much fun without Brendan.

The phone rang again, and she allowed herself the crazy wish that it was Brendan calling to say he'd changed his mind and Charlie Donovan could just walk to Shadrach because seeing her was much more important.

The voice was male, but it wasn't Brendan's. "This is Graham Lucas. Is this Maxie?"

Graham Lucas? Why was he calling *her*?

Maxie didn't know what to say. If he knew Candie was fine, that she was feeling well enough to attend the party, he'd show up there and make her crazy. "Why are you calling *me*, Graham?"

"I wasn't sure Candie would talk to me. Sometimes she won't. And I needed to know that she was okay. I heard about what happened and I haven't seen her on campus, so I was worried."

But Candie doesn't *want* you worrying about her, Maxie thought but didn't say. "She's better," she said cautiously. "So you can quit worrying."

There was distress in his voice as he said, "Why was she home that night? She wasn't supposed to be."

Maxie wasn't sure she'd heard him correctly. "What? What night?"

"The night it happened. That food poisoning. I asked her out to dinner that night, and she said she couldn't go because she already had a dinner date. So when I first heard about what happened, I figured she was okay, since she wasn't planning on eating at the house. But then, I didn't see her on campus, so I asked someone and they said she was in the hospital. I couldn't believe it. She wasn't supposed to *be* there. Why *was* she?"

Maxie rolled her eyes heavenward. Because she lied to you, you twit. You wouldn't leave her alone when she told you the truth, so she lied. I don't blame her. Aloud, she said, "Maybe her date was canceled, Graham. Anyway, she's better, so relax, okay?"

"I can't help it." Now who was whining? "We

had a fight the other day and all I could think of when I heard about this rotten business was that I might not get the chance to make up with her, tell her I was sorry."

She almost felt sorry for Graham. If only he'd take the hint and buzz off. Disappear. But he was clinging to Candie like fungus, just like she'd said.

"Maybe you should play hard to get, Graham," she offered, taking pity on him.

"What?"

"Never mind." The concept was probably foreign to him. "Like I said, Candie's fine. Gotta go, Graham. Bye."

Well, at least she'd saved Candie a conversation Candie didn't want to have.

She was just about to switch on the hairdryer when the doorbell rang.

What now?

Ignore it, she told herself, whoever it is will go away.

Then she remembered that Mildred had informed them that morning that the university was planning to have the house painted, now that the weather had warmed up. Maxie had initially objected, feeling that this wasn't a good time for such activity around the house. But she had quickly realized, on second thought, that having a crew of painters stationed outside might not be such a bad idea.

"Every member of the crew," Mildred told the girls, "will, of course, be thoroughly checked out by the administration and probably by the police, as well. So having them around might actually make us all feel just a tiny bit safer. And, of course," she had added cheerfully, "our lovely house will soon be wearing a fresh new coat of paint."

Maybe the person ringing the front doorbell was here about the painting job.

Brring, brring, brring.

The noise was driving Maxie nuts. Whoever it was wasn't going to go away. Besides, it could be someone who lived in the house and had forgotten their key. The door was kept locked at all times now.

Wrapping her white terrycloth robe tightly around her, she ran down the stairs. She had the peephole and the chain lock. It wasn't as if she was about to let anyone *in*. If it wasn't someone who belonged at Omega house, she'd just get rid of them.

She peered through the peephole. Her eyes widened in disbelief, and her mouth dropped open.

She couldn't believe what she was seeing.

Leaving the chain lock on, she pulled the door open a few inches.

Chapter 14

Standing on the porch was one of the strangest-looking people Maxie had ever seen. She was a tall, heavyset woman with an unbelievable amount of cranberry-colored hair piled high on her head and hanging loose, in tight Shirley Temple curls, around her face. The eyes, behind Coke-bottle-thick eyeglasses, were heavily made-up with false eyelashes and several shades of fluorescent shadow that hurt Maxie's eyes. Her wide, generous mouth was outlined with dark brown liner and filled in with several layers of glossy, bright pink lipstick.

"Yes?" Maxie asked when the initial shock had passed. She bit her lower lip to keep from smiling at the garish lime-green wide-legged pants and the hot-pink and lime-green flowered sweatshirt spilling out from beneath the woman's open denim jacket. "Can I help you?"

"Well, sweetie," the woman boomed in a

loud, brassy voice, "you sure can. You can deliver me, posthaste, to Mrs. Allison Barre's baby daughter, Candace. I'm Tia Maria, the one and only, and I'm here to make little Candie the work of art that nature intended her to be. I'm here on her mama's say-so, so you'd best let me in, hon. Allie, I mean Mrs. Barre, will *not* be in a generous mood if I don't transform her precious darlin'. And if Mrs. Barre isn't feeling generous, this sorority doesn't get its semi-annual whopping, whale-sized checks, if you get my drift."

Maxie was speechless. "Tia Maria?"

"You got it. My orders are to make Allie's precious darling look good enough to knock every hormone-crazed young man on campus off his Reeboks. So how's about letting me in, sweetie, so I can get to work."

Candie's mother's hairdresser. This was the woman Candie's mother had told them so many stories about the day she came for the tea.

"Here's my card, hon." The woman held out a shocking-pink business card, embossed with her name and, directly underneath that the words, BEAUTIFIER PAR EXCELLENCE.

Maxie couldn't help smiling.

Tia Maria said proudly, "I do faces, too. Not just hair. Faces."

Not the same way you do your own, I hope, Maxie thought.

"No one's home right now," Maxie said, making up her mind and releasing the chain lock. "I don't know how soon they'll all be back, but you can come in and wait. You can wait in my room, and keep me company."

"Well, thanks, hon," Tia Maria said, hefting her black leather case and giving Maxie a broad, pink-lipsticked smile. "Don't mind if I do. My tootsies are giving out."

Maxie pulled the door open, and the hairdresser stepped inside.

In her room, Maxie motioned Tia Maria to a wicker chair at the desk and went to the dresser to pick up her hairbrush.

"Listen, hon, I have a great idea," Tia Maria said, not sitting down. "Since Allie's baby girl isn't here at this precise moment, what say you and me have us a makeover session? On my honor, I can make you so gorgeous you'll think the Body-Snatchers came and replaced the original you with some famous movie star. How about it?"

"A makeover? Me?" Maxie glanced around nervously.

The woman read her mind. "Oh, relax, sweetie," she said, waving jewelled hands in

Maxie's face. "Now just sit right there and let me get to work."

What the heck, Maxie figured as she sat down in front of the dresser. It might be fun, being made over. She could always undo whatever Tia Maria did if it was really awful.

While Tia Maria worked, she talked. Nonstop. She set Maxie's hair on hot rollers, talking the whole time about politics, religion, child-rearing, and the state of the nation in general, all in that brassy, booming voice. By the time she started on Maxie's face, Maxie's ears were ringing.

She worked quickly, efficiently. Maxie admired the way her fingers, in thin plastic gloves, flew, and how the brushes she used seemed to fit so perfectly in her hand, as if they were a part of it.

"And you poor guys here," Tia Maria said as she brushed Maxie's brows upward in firm but gentle strokes and applied tiny dabs of vaseline to hold the hairs in place, "you've really been having a time of it, haven't you?"

At first, Maxie thought she was talking about something political, like state budget cuts that had affected the university, or a recent hike in tuition.

"I mean," the hairdresser continued, nimble fingers applying blush high on Maxie's cheekbones, "first, those things being stolen and then the ants in the pantry, yuck! And that poor kid tumbling into the fountain, and then of course, that dreadful insecticide. You girls were really lucky there. Could have been all she wrote, don't you think? Beats me what the world is coming to."

Maxie froze in her chair. Her eyes went to the mirror in front of her. Every nerve in her body sprang to attention as she watched Tia Maria bend to fill a huge, fluffy brush with loose translucent powder and then stand to shake off the excess. Maxie couldn't think, couldn't sort things out . . . something bad had just happened and she had to concentrate, so that she could figure out exactly what it was.

Yes, now she had it. How . . . how . . .

"How did you know about all of that?" she demanded. She had let this woman into Omega house. Without seeing any identification except for a stupid bright-pink business card. Not enough. Not nearly enough proof that she was who she said she was.

"Oh, Allie told me," the hairdresser said breezily. "Clients tell me everything. You'd think I was their best friend or sister or something."

Maxie sat perfectly still, not even wincing when Tia Maria began pulling the hot rollers from her hair and had to pull sharply on one that had become slightly tangled. That explanation made sense. Allison Barre might very well have told her hairdresser everything that had happened lately at her daughter's sorority house.

There was only one problem with that explanation. There was only one reason Maxie still hadn't relaxed, her stomach hadn't stopped churning, her hands trembled in her lap.

She hadn't relaxed because she knew, she *knew* that Candie had never *told* her mother about any of that stuff. She wouldn't have. Candie had said that her mother would never believe her, never. That her mother would more readily believe that Candie, a straight-A student, was suddenly flunking all of her courses before she'd believe anything negative about Omega Phi.

Then how . . . if that were so . . . how did Tia Maria know . . . ?

The last hot roller had been removed. Tia Maria began to brush, swiftly and thoroughly, Maxie's shoulder-length brown hair. One hand held the brush, the other firmly held Maxie's head still.

Would a woman whose profession was making other women beautiful really do such an inexpert, outlandish job when she made up her own face?

Was the garish makeup Tia Maria was wearing really just her style?

Or . . . was it a disguise? No one could possibly figure out what the woman *really* looked like underneath all that makeup.

Maxie's heart thudded down into her kneecaps. Oh, God, she thought miserably, I fell for it. I fell for her whole stupid routine. I don't *believe* this. How could I be so *dumb*? Now I'm alone in the house with someone who should *not* know anything about what's been going on here. . . . but *does*. *Someone who isn't who she says she is*. There is only *one* way this person could know what happened in this house. She had to have something to do with all of it. What am I going to do?

What she *wasn't* going to do, she decided when her brain finally roused itself enough to think clearly, was let on that she suspected anything. All she had to do was make up some excuse to leave the room, slip down the stairs and run outside. Whoever this *was*, standing behind her brushing her hair, still prattling on and on about how awful it must have been for all of them, wouldn't be dumb enough to do anything to her once she was outside, where people could *see*. If Tuttle's truck was in the driveway, she'd race over there and use his phone to call the police. If he wasn't . . .

She'd worry about that when she got outside.

"Tia Maria," Maxie said, willing her voice to remain perfectly steady, "could we take a break for a sec? I think that I forgot to lock the door when I let you in, and the rule now is that the door has to be locked at all times." She forced a smile. "Since you know what's been going on, I'm sure you'll agree the rule makes sense, right?"

"Absolutely, hon." The hand on the side of Maxie's head didn't ease. "But you *did* lock it. I saw you. So relax."

"No, I . . ."

The hand tightened. "It's *locked*."

She knows, Maxie thought. She knows that I know. *Now* how am I going to get away from her?

The person behind her had made Cath fall off the fountain wall. She couldn't have known that Cath wouldn't be killed in that fall. And she had, by her own admission just now, done something with insecticide, whether the police had found evidence of that or not, that had sent many of Maxie's friends to the hospital writhing in pain. Again, she couldn't have known that they wouldn't die. Maybe she had even been hoping that they would.

So, although Maxie didn't add the word "alive" to her question, it was there, dancing around in her head, tormenting her, taunting her . . .

How am I going to get away from her *alive*?

Chapter 15

Maxie's mind raced along with her frantic pulse. Where *was* everyone? It was almost six o'clock. Weren't they coming back for dinner?

Maxie felt totally abandoned.

Think, think . . . make the hairdresser think she's mistaken, that you really don't know anything at all, you're not suspicious . . . then she'll let down her guard so you can get away before . . . before *what*? Don't think about it.

"The police didn't find any insecticide in the spaghetti we ate that night," Maxie said, in a casual tone of voice that anyone would use in an ordinary, everyday conversation. It took great effort.

"Well, of course not," Tia Maria's voice boomed. "It wouldn't *be* in the spaghetti, darlin'. Too easy to trace. Anyone with any brains would simply spray the stuff on the plates while they were sittin' on the dining room table, before any food was on them. Then it'd get mixed in with what was eaten, but once the plates were washed, who'd know?"

Maxie's heart fluttered. She had something concrete to take to the police now. If she ever got the chance to *go* to the police.

Tia Maria, hairbrush in hand, moved to Maxie's left side.

The black cord from the hot rollers was still plugged in. It draped its way down from the top of the dresser to an electrical outlet near Maxie's feet. And it was hanging between Maxie and the hairdresser, a thick black snake separating them.

The door out of the bedroom was to Maxie's right.

"I mean," Tia Maria amended, as if aware that she had said too much, "that's how I figured someone did it. When Allie told me about it."

Allie *never* told you about it, Maxie thought angrily, and with Tia Maria's fingers still in her hair, she took a deep breath, let it out, and dove sideways, to her right, yelping in pain as several strands of hair were left in Tia Maria's hand. She hit the floor ready to run, scrambling to her feet as an astonished Tia Maria yelled, "Hey!" and dove after her.

And tripped over the cord from the hot rollers.

Tia Maria was flung forward, thrown face-first into the hard wooden chair that Maxie, only a split-second before, had been sitting in.

Feet flying, Maxie ran. Out of the room, down the hall, down the stairs . . . no one there . . . sounds of footsteps on the stairs . . . chasing her . . . the feet behind her moved quickly for someone as big as the hairdresser . . .

To the front door, fumbling with the chain lock. Shouldn't have slipped it back into place after letting the hairdresser in, too late now. . . .

Behind her, the heavy feet, pounding, pounding too close. . . . no time to open two locks . . . run, *run!*

Maxie ran into the dining room, slammed the swinging door shut behind her, thrust a heavy dining room chair against it. It wouldn't stop the person who *wasn't* Tia Maria, but it might slow her down.

Hide. Should hide. Back door has two locks on it, not enough time to unlatch both before heavy hands would be on her throat, choking the very life out of it . . . have to hide . . .

Where?

The sound of a heavy chair falling to the floor in the dining room, a hinge screaming in protest as the swinging door was flung open.

Right behind her, right behind her . . .

The pantry? No. No back door. No way out. She'd be trapped in there like an animal in a cage.

There! Beside the kitchen pantry door. The laundry chute. The small window swinging inward a foot up from the floor. Was she small enough to crawl in there? Yes.

If she threw herself in, willy-nilly, she'd fall, fall to the basement below. But if she didn't break both legs, she could get out the basement door and run for help.

No time to think. Turn around, crawl in quickly, backwards, try to slide down the chute slowly, carefully, maybe holding onto the sides. Was there anything to hold onto on the sides of the chute?

Maxie spun around, threw herself into the chute backwards, feet and legs hanging down behind her. But instead of letting herself fall, her hands fastened themselves onto the wooden frame at the top of the chute as the little door swung shut. She hung on for dear life, unwilling to let go and slide down into the darkness below.

She was hidden. If Tia Maria didn't know about the laundry chute, she might not notice it. Maybe she'd give up, leave the house. Go away.

Begone, Maxie thought giddily, begone!

The telephone shrilled, once, twice, three times, four . . . Maxie yearned to crawl out and answer it, scream into it for help. But she didn't dare.

Footsteps in the kitchen. Voice bellowing, "Where the hell are you, you little witch?"

Don't look in here, Maxie prayed, don't notice the chute, let your false eyelashes get in the way and don't notice the chute. Her fingers ached from clinging to the narrow strip of molding. She would have to let go soon. If she could only hold on until she heard the footsteps leaving the kitchen, so the hairdresser wouldn't hear her landing in the cellar and come looking for her there . . .

Suddenly, one foot, the left, felt colder than the right foot.

Maxie glanced over her shoulder, kicking the left foot upward at the same time.

Oh, no, it was *bare*! No white terrycloth slipper. Had the slipper dropped off while she was hanging there? Or had it . . . had it dropped off when she was climbing into the chute? Was it even now lying just outside the little swinging door, screaming her location to her hunter?

Please, she prayed, tears of terror gathering

in her eyes, please let that slipper be down in the cellar where no one can see it.

No such luck. "Gotcha!" a voice boomed from only inches beyond the chute's door, telling Maxie the slipper was not in the cellar. It had just been discovered in the kitchen, pointing the way to her hiding place.

Maxie stopped breathing, couldn't breathe, couldn't. The blood in her veins stopped rushing as if it had been dammed somewhere in her body. Let *go*! an inner voice ordered, let *go*! Drop to the basement, take your chances on a broken leg or ankle, and do it *now*!

But her fingers were frozen in place.

The door swung inward, slapping into her face. A large, strong hand reached in and grabbed her wrist.

She screamed.

And, as if in answer to her scream, a car door slammed outside. Then another. Footsteps on the cement walk outside, voices . . . talking, laughing.

The hand on her wrist froze.

Feet shuffled backward uncertainly.

Then, a muffled oath, the hand on her wrist flew away, the swinging chute door dropped back into place, and feet scuttled away, toward the back door.

The sound of the back door opening and closing came at exactly the same moment as the wonderful sound of the front door opening, and afterward Maxie couldn't have said which sound was more welcome to her ears.

The phony Tia Maria was gone.

Her friends were home.

She was safe.

She could crawl from the chute into the kitchen, tell her story, call the police . . . she was *safe*.

And even as she thought that, her fingers, numb from holding onto the thin wooden molding, released their grip.

By the time she realized what was happening, it was too late.

Her hands slid free of the doorframe and her body slid, feet first, down the long wooden chute like a child on a playground toy, to the hard basement floor waiting below.

Chapter 16

Relax your legs right *now*, an inner voice commanded as Maxie whizzed down the laundry chute, or the bones will shatter when you land. Pretend you've fainted.

Obeying, Maxie went limp.

Just in time. Although she flew out onto the basement's cold stone floor and landed in a heap, there were no sharp cracking sounds as she hit. There was only her own sudden yipe of pain as her left ankle twisted cruelly sideways beneath her.

She lay perfectly still in the darkness, her breath coming in short, painful gasps.

She wasn't dead.

She wasn't even unconscious.

And none of her bones hurt enough to be broken, although the ankle was iffy.

Above her in the kitchen, she heard voices.

The relief she felt was overwhelming, turning her body to jelly. She would call to them and they would come to rescue her.

Maxie opened her mouth to shout and at that precise moment a red-hot pain shot up her leg from the ankle to the hip. The pain was so intense, she gasped. Although she fought against the ensuing wave of dizziness that assailed her, it was too strong for her. With her mouth still open to shout, and a look of dismay on her face, she slid into unconsciousness.

When she awoke, she was in her own bed, in her own room, and she was surrounded by people. They were all there, looking down upon her with concern: Erica, Tinker, Candie, Mildred, Chloe . . .

As she opened her eyes, they began bombarding her with questions. Mildred wanted to know what had happened in her room, why the chair was tipped over, the hot rollers spilled across the floor, and was she all right? Erica and Tinker wanted to know what she'd been doing in the basement and was she all right? And Chloe asked her what her slipper was doing in the kitchen and was she all right?

"Something is very wrong with that ankle," Mildred said sternly. "I've called a doctor and he's agreed to come here to see you. I don't want any more ambulances rushing up to our door if it's not absolutely necessary." She

143

peered down at Maxie. "You don't have a really bad headache or anything, do you?"

"No, no headache." Maxie tried to sit up, but the pain in her ankle stopped her. "And I don't think my ankle's broken. I didn't hear anything snap when I fell out of the laundry chute."

"The laundry chute?" Mildred looked blank.

"Mrs. B.," Maxie said wearily, "I think you'd better call the police."

She really couldn't tell the officers very much. Underneath the thick glasses and the weird cranberry-colored hair and the layers of makeup, "Tia Maria" could have been anyone. Anyone at all.

Well . . . not just *anyone*. "She knew about the things that have been going on here at the house," Maxie told the officer armed with a notebook. "Not that many people know the details, but *she* did. And she said there *was* insecticide in what we ate that night, but according to her, it was on the plates, not in the food."

"You keep saying 'she'," one of the officers said. "You're sure it was a woman?"

Maxie thought for a moment. The doctor had given her something for the pain in her ankle, which had turned out not to be broken, but badly sprained. The painkiller was strong, and she was exhausted, and it was hard to think clearly. "Yeah, I guess," she said drowsily. "She was pretty big. I guess it could have been a guy."

"Well, you get some rest," the same officer said kindly. "Tomorrow we'll want a list of everyone you girls might have told about the previous incidents. We'll check those people out."

When they had gone and Tinker, Erica, and Candie had settled on Tinker's bed to keep Maxie company until she fell asleep, they discussed who had known about Tia Maria and who they'd told about the nasty goings-on at the house.

Maxie struggled to think clearly. Brendan and Jenna knew what had happened, of course, because she'd told them. Had she also told them about Tia Maria? She thought that she had, although it was hard to remember now.

Candie, Tinker, and Erica all reluctantly admitted that they'd told more than one person about Tia Maria. "She sounded like such a character," Erica admitted.

"I didn't tell Graham Lucas," Candie said thoughtfully, "but he was sitting in the next booth at Vinnie's when I was telling a bunch of people about her. I remember being really annoyed by that because I thought he was eavesdropping. I still do."

And Tinker pointed out that most of campus probably knew all of the details of every incident that had taken place at the sorority house. "Even if we hadn't told people," she said, "you know how that stuff gets around. Cath told me *everyone* knew what was going on at Nightmare Hall when things were so bad. She *hated* that."

"Thanks for rescuing me," Maxie said. Her eyelids suddenly weighed a ton. "How long was I down in the basement, anyway? Aren't you guys missing the Tri-Delt party?" She didn't care that she wasn't going. Brendan wasn't going to be there. He'd driven some guy somewhere . . .

"Longer than you *should* have been," Tinker said guiltily. "No one noticed your slipper until we'd all been home a while. I'm sorry, Maxie. Erica found it there by the chute, and then Candie came downstairs and said your room was a mess, so we knew something was wrong. That's when we started looking for you. It was my idea," she added proudly, "to check the basement where the chute comes out."

"And we don't care about the party," Erica added. "The Tri-Delts don't give such a great party, anyway."

They were still laughing when Maxie quit struggling against sleep and closed her eyes.

She was disappointed because there was something really, really important that she needed to remember. But she couldn't . . . couldn't . . .

On Sunday, they handed over to the police their lists of who might have known about Tia Maria *and* the incidents that had taken place in the house. The officers' faces fell when they saw the length of the lists.

"Is there anyone on campus who *didn't* know?" one said. But they took the lists and left.

Later that day, Cath was released from the hospital. She hadn't been home more than an hour when she came into Maxie's room to announce that she was leaving. Leaving the house, leaving Omega Phi Delta. Erica, Tinker, and Candie were stationed on Tinker's bed.

Cath had a cast on her arm and she walked stiffly, telling them her back still hurt. "Thanks for pledging me," she said quietly, standing in the center of the room, "but I've decided to go back to Nightmare Hall." Her pale cheeks flushed. "I've . . . I've missed my friends there. I guess it's not such a good idea to leave the place you've been living, in the middle of a semester. Too hard to get used to. I'm really sorry," Cath added, and left.

A chagrined silence followed her departure.

We all know the real reason she's leaving, Maxie told herself, and we're embarrassed that Cath thinks Omega house is even scarier now than that gloomy old place down the road. Omega house scarier than Nightmare Hall? How was that possible?

This last Sunday in the month of March was turning out to be the gloomiest day of Maxie's life.

"I talked to my mother," Candie said. "I didn't tell her anything that had happened, of course, she'd go ballistic on me, but I managed, very cleverly, I thought, to find out what Tia Maria looks like."

"And . . . ?" Maxie sat up in her bed.

"She's only five feet, four inches tall and she has short platinum blonde hair and blue eyes. And she doesn't wear glasses. Or, according to my mother, lime green. Ever."

So the real Tia Maria was a far cry from the person who had been standing on the front porch when Maxie opened the door on Friday. Maxie wasn't really surprised. "I should have known," she said miserably. "I should have known someone as classy as your mother wouldn't have a hairdresser who looked like something out of a cartoon."

"Quit beating yourself over the head," Erica said. "I personally think that any one of us would have let the woman in. We'd heard so much about Tia Maria from Candie's mom, we all felt like we knew her. Whoever that was pretending to be her, it was a brilliant idea, if you ask me."

Brendan called later that afternoon. "How was the party?" he wanted to know. He hadn't heard what had happened. She didn't want him to know, which was exactly why she hadn't called him.

"Didn't go. You weren't going to be there, so I opted to stay home." She wasn't really lying. She *had* decided to stay home. Of course, she'd had a little help deciding. . . .

"Gee, I'm flattered. So, you feel like canoeing this afternoon? Not a bad day out there."

The trouble with telling one little white lie was that you just dug yourself a hole. She hadn't told him about her ankle, so now she had no excuse for not going canoeing.

Maybe a half-truth would do. "Can't. Went and turned my stupid ankle yesterday. I'm stuck in bed." Stupid, stupid, she scolded . . . if he found out from someone else exactly *how* she had "turned" her ankle, he'd be furious that she hadn't told him the whole story.

He was properly sympathetic, said he understood, and he'd call her later.

She felt guilty when she replaced the receiver, but she also felt relieved that they hadn't got into another why-don't-you-leave-that-dangerous-place-immediately argument. She wasn't in the mood.

She didn't tell Jenna the whole truth when she called later that night, either. But Jenna was much more suspicious. "What do you mean, you turned your ankle? Turned it into what?"

"Into a black-and-blue, swollen mess, that's what."

"How? And does this mean you're going to be out of commission all weekend?"

"I . . . I fell in the basement." That was almost true. Except the correct word would have been "in*to*" the basement. "And yeah, it does mean I'm pretty much stuck in my bed."

"Well, I'll just saunter on over there, then, keep you company. What are friends for?"

"No!" Maxie immediately regretted shouting out the word. But Jenna was much too aware, too smart, to be allowed inside Omega house now. The minute she saw how gloomy everyone was, how oddly quiet the place was, she'd know in a second that something was very, very wrong. Besides, someone might accidentally let the truth slip out. "I mean, that's really sweet of you, but I hit my head, too, and I've got this excruciating headache, so I'm just going to sleep, okay?"

There was a hurt silence on the other end of the line. Then, stiffly, "Yeah, sure I get it. Not to worry. Sleep it off, okay? I'm sure all your sisters will be tending to your every whim, just like sisters should. Talk to you later." And Jenna hung up.

She doesn't believe me, Maxie thought as the line went dead. She probably doesn't even believe I actually hurt my ankle.

Some people seemed to lie so easily. Other people, like Maximilia McKeon, were lousy at it. Had to be a genetic thing.

By Monday, Maxie was able to hobble around the upstairs hall, gingerly limping along on her Ace-bandaged ankle.

She was passing Candie's room, the door open, when she heard from behind the closed door, "I just want to know where you were Saturday night, that's all. Humor me, okay, Graham? Just *tell* me?"

Maxie rapped on the door.

Candie, the phone to her ear, waved her inside. "Alone?" she said into the phone. "You went to the movies alone Saturday night? What did you see?"

Maxie sank gratefully into Candie's desk

chair, propping her injured ankle up on the edge of the bed.

"No, this isn't an inquisition. I'm taking a survey . . . on what students do on weekends, that's all. For . . . for soc class. It's due this morning." Candie grinned at Maxie. Then she listened for a few seconds, and said, "Just because I called you for my survey, Graham, doesn't mean I've changed my mind about going out with you. Like I said before, when there's a nuclear war and you're the only other human being left on earth, not a minute before. Thanks for the info." She hung up, a satisfied smile on her face.

"You shouldn't be so rude to him, Candie. I saw how angry he was with you that day on campus. He's got a temper, and you're just baiting him."

"It doesn't matter now." Candie sat down on the bed, careful to avoid jarring Maxie's ankle. "Listen," she said eagerly, "I knew Graham never went to the Tri-Delt party because I called over there and asked. Suzy Cummings said he wasn't there, she was positive. So I wanted to know where he was, right? So I called him. He said he went to a movie, by himself. Have you ever in your life seen Graham Lucas anywhere alone? Except when he's driving me nuts, I mean?"

"No." It was true. Graham didn't seem to like being alone. He was always with a bunch of friends, but never by himself.

"Me, either. And I don't believe for a second that he went to the movies alone Saturday night. Which means," Candie said triumphantly, "that he could have been *here*."

"Here?"

"You said the phony Tia Maria was tall and had wide shoulders, right? Well, Graham's tall and has wide shoulders. Why couldn't it have been him?"

"Candie, why would Graham want to hurt me?"

"It's not *you* he wanted to hurt," Candie said impatiently. "It's this sorority. When I first started turning him down, I used stuff that was going on here as an excuse. It really made him mad after a while. He started making cracks about this place, about how we all stuck together and didn't want anyone else in our lives. Like . . . like he was jealous."

Just like Brendan, Maxie thought. And even Jenna.

She thought about that for a minute. Graham behind all that makeup and cranberry-colored hair? Possible. He was the right size.

"I'm going to nose around," Candie promised. "See if I can find out anything about Graham that we could take to the police. Want to help?"

Maxie shook her head. "I'm no detective. Let the police handle it, Candie. If Graham *is* the person who pretended to be Tia Maria, he's dangerous." Remembering that iron grip on her wrist as she hung suspended in the laundry chute, she shuddered. "Stay away from him, Candie. Promise me."

"Okay, okay, relax!"

Maxie suppressed a wild urge to laugh. Relax? *Relax?*

Not in *this* house.

Chapter 17

The house painters arrived early on Monday morning, setting up an intricate scaffolding system on one side of the house. A thick wooden platform supported by fat white crisscrossed rungs resembling monkey bars in a playground, it held the painters high above the ground as they scraped away the old paint. When Maxie arrived home and sat in the kitchen soaking her throbbing ankle, she found the sound of their tools comforting. As Mildred had said, having people outside, especially people who had been carefully checked out by the university security force, made her feel safer. Who would be stupid enough to try anything with half a dozen men and women surrounding the house?

The person who had chased her through the house and sent her into that laundry chute was not that stupid. Disguising his or her true identity as Tia Maria had been a stroke of brilliance, as far as Maxie was concerned. Crazy, yes, stupid, no.

Erica had called a meeting for after dinner. When they were all seated on couches, chairs, and the floor in the living room, she asked if anyone had any idea who might be tormenting the residents of the Omega Phi house.

"The messenger who returned our stolen property was the real thing," she said in a somber tone of voice, "but none of the other people who've visited the house lately were. The doctor, the first exterminator, and the hairdresser, were all fakes. And," glancing at Maxie, sitting with her foot propped up on the edge of Tinker's chair, "Maxie thinks there was a phony catering staff member, too. This is no joke, guys, and we need to come up with some answers. Any ideas, anybody?"

"A bunch of girls we rushed, but didn't pledge?" Candie suggested. "They could have formed their own nasty little club and worked out a sick plan of revenge."

"Right," Tinker agreed. "I know how *that* feels. You get all excited and have all these fantasies about what it will be like to be an Omega, and then boom! you find out you didn't measure up, after all. You lay awake nights wondering what you did wrong. . . ." Seeing

Maxie's shocked gaze on her, Tinker flushed and added quickly, "That's why I was so happy when I *did* get in. But there are lots of others who didn't."

I never knew she felt that way, Maxie was thinking. She never told me.

Erica nodded. "We've already thought of that, and the police have that list. As you all know, I was dead set against involving the police, but I have to admit now it was the right thing to do. They're checking out those girls now. Anyone else have any ideas? Anybody dump a boyfriend lately? Especially a dumpee who didn't take it very well? He might have enlisted the aid of some of his friends."

Everyone looked in Candie's direction.

"I didn't *dump* Graham," she protested. "I . . . discouraged him. Not the same thing at all. Besides," she added with a derisive laugh, "Graham Lucas is afraid of his own shadow. That's why he hangs out in groups most of the time."

But Maxie was remembering the argument she'd witnessed on campus between Candie and Graham. He hadn't looked the least bit afraid. He'd looked *angry. Very* angry.

"There's another possibility," Tinker volunteered. "We all know that some people on campus think we're snobs. We've all heard comments. They think we look down on anyone who isn't in a fraternity or sorority. Maybe one of us has a friend from before we pledged who feels left out now and is angry about it."

Maxie felt her cheeks grow warm as images of Brendan and Jenna flew into her mind. But Brendan was okay with her sorority life now, wasn't he? And Jenna would never, never hurt anyone. Or would she?

"I know you guys don't want to think that way," Tinker added softly, "but Cath and Maxie both could have been *killed*. Think about that, okay? Nothing can happen while the house is being painted, with the painters here all the time, but when they're done . . ."

They all knew only too well that once the painters left, they'd be on their own again.

"Well," Erica finished, "if any of you come up with someone you think the police should be checking out, let me know, okay? It's important. For all of us."

"Besides," Tinker pointed out as they all got up and pushed their chairs in, "the painters leave at seven o'clock every day. That means we're fair game from seven on."

"The police are stepping up their patrols from seven to eleven," Erica said. "But it's still up to us to come up with some answers about who's doing this. Put your thinking caps on, okay, and don't let your loyalty to friends or old boyfriends get in the way. We all have to think about what's best for our sisters."

Maxie knew Erica was right. Maybe, she thought then, I should tell someone about the wig I found in Jenna's bathroom.

But Jenna had explained that. Little Orphan Annie, right? That wig certainly wasn't the one the phony Tia Maria had been wearing, anyway. Although, if you knew where to get one wig, you could get another. You could always dye it a cranberry color yourself.

During the evenings all that week, the house emptied out the minute the painting crew had gone. No one was keen on staying in the house during those hours when their mock security force had left for the day. Suddenly, the library or Vinnie's or Burgers Etc. or the radio station in the Tower or a friend's dorm room or the mall seemed infinitely safer than Omega house.

But Maxie's ankle was too swollen after a day of hobbling around campus to allow her to leave the house. If Tinker didn't stay home and keep her company, Erica or Candie did. Sometimes all three stayed, and they ate popcorn and Oreos and studied and talked and laughed and played music, just as if their lives hadn't been turned upside down.

Maxie would try to pretend that life was just

as it had been ever since she moved into Omega house. Nothing had changed. All of that had just been a bad nightmare, and now it was over.

But it didn't work. There was always a reminder, like her throbbing ankle, or the ruby ring on Candie's finger or the pearl earrings Erica was wearing, or the hot rollers sitting out on the dresser, reminding her of the fake Tia Maria.

The nightmare wasn't over.

The police had found no fingerprints in Maxie and Tinker's room. Tia Maria had worn plastic gloves.

Jenna and Brendan were on the list Maxie had given to the police, the list of people who knew about everything that had happened and knew about Tia Maria. She hadn't wanted to write down their names. But they *knew*. So she'd had no choice.

Would the police question them? They'd be angry, knowing they might be suspects. Graham Lucas wouldn't like it, either. But he was on those lists, too.

Wednesday, she was trudging across campus against a chilly, late-March wind, when Charlie Donovan flagged her down near the fountain on the commons.

"Seen Brendan?" he asked. His round, freckled face was red with cold.

"No." She'd hardly talked to Brendan at all since the night of the Tri-Delt party. He had called her on Sunday and said he was busy with arrangements for an April Fool's party scheduled for that Friday night in the student center. It was being sponsored by the Young Democrats club on campus. Brendan was the group's vice president. He had said he probably wouldn't have much time to party, but he'd take her home. She hadn't talked to him since.

She could hardly complain about how busy he was now, when she'd disappointed him so many times because of sorority activities.

"How was your sister's engagement party?" she asked as she and Charlie began to walk toward the dining hall at Lester, intent on lunch.

"Beats me," he said. "I never got there. Boy, was my mom on the warpath when she found out I wasn't going to make it. You'd think I'd done it on purpose."

Maxie's steps slowed. "You didn't go to the party? But I thought Brendan was taking you."

"He was." Charlie held the door to Lester open for Maxie. "Good old Brendan was going to haul me over the hill to Shadrach, but at the last minute, he called and said he couldn't get his car to start. It was too late to ask someone else, so . . . anyway, it worked out okay. I had a paper to turn in on Monday and if I'd gone to the party, I wouldn't have finished it. When my mom started in on me for disappointing Lucy, that's my sister, I said, 'Well, mom, which would you rather have, a son who's nice to his sister or a son who's a college graduate?' She didn't seem to think that was very funny. She'll get over it."

Maxie wasn't listening. They went into the dining hall and she walked through the line with Charlie. She selected a tuna salad sandwich, a small salad, and a piece of carrot cake, but she was hardly aware of what she was doing.

Brendan hadn't gone to Shadrach Saturday night? Why hadn't he told her that? Why hadn't he called and told her he could go to the Tri-Delt party when he found out he was going to be in town, after all?

If he had, she wouldn't have ended up in the cellar with a sprained ankle.

Not fair. Brendan couldn't have known that was happening to her at Omega house. But he'd never told her that his plans had changed that night.

She saw Jenna sitting in the corner with two other girls, and waved.

Jenna smiled and waved. After a few minutes, she picked up her tray and walked across the room to sit down opposite Maxie. Charlie said hi, then excused himself to go join some friends at another table.

"Did you go to the Tri-Delt party Saturday night?" Maxie asked abruptly when she had assured Jenna that her ankle was better.

"Me? Are you kidding? Why would I want to do that?"

"Oh, come off it, Jenna. You've been to sorority parties lots of times. And you always have fun, so quit pretending you think sororities are only one step up from witches' covens."

Jenna grinned. "Okay, so I went. So sue me. And yeah, actually, I did have a good time. Met this real cute guy. Guess what his name is?"

"Biff."

"No, but close. It's Skip."

Maxie hooted. "You're dating someone named Skippy? *Skippy?*"

Jenna's round cheeks flushed scarlet. "Not Skippy," she said hotly, "Skip! Real name, Howard. Howard Ulysses Porter."

"No wonder they call him Skip. Fraternity guy?"

The flush deepened. "Afraid so. Sigma Chi. And don't say a word, Maximilia McKeon, or I'll slap you with my corn fritter. Frat brat or not, he's cute and he's got a brain. Can't beat that. And he doesn't care that I'm not in a sorority."

"Why should he? *You* have more hang-ups about that than anyone else does. Listen, Jenna, I'm thrilled about your new romance, really, I am, but was Brendan at that party?"

"Brendan? Without you? Would Homer be there without Marge? Would Abbott be there without Costello? Would Isabella Sands be there without makeup? No to all of the above."

"He wasn't there?"

"Nope. Why?"

"I . . . I just wondered, that's all."

They agreed to meet at the April Fool's party on Friday night. "You'll like Skip," Jenna said happily. "And if you don't, keep it to yourself. Nobody cares." But she laughed as she said it.

The wig really *was* part of her Orphan Annie costume, Maxie thought with relief as she watched Jenna leave, a new bounce in her step. But then, I always knew that . . . *didn't* I?

It occurred to her then that out of everything that had happened, the worst thing by far was the mistrust. It ate away inside of you, like a worm burrowing through an apple.

And now she needed to know why Brendan hadn't told her he wasn't going to Shadrach, after all.

"I did call," he said when he called her that night and she asked him that very question. "Nobody answered."

The phone . . . ringing when she was hanging in the laundry chute.

"I figured you'd probably left early, a bunch of you, going out to eat first or something, and you'd go on to the party with other people."

"Why didn't you go to the party, then? If you thought I was there."

She could almost hear his shrug. "Had to work on my car. Got it running, finally, but it was too late to take Donovan to his sister's party. So I hit the books for a while and then sacked out. And when I called you and you said you didn't go to the party, I didn't see any point in telling you I hadn't gone to Shadrach." After a moment, he said, "Why all the questions? Anything wrong?"

A lot of things are wrong, she thought, but she didn't feel like getting into it. "No. Charlie said you guys didn't go to his sister's party, and then Jenna said you weren't at the other party, either, so I just wondered what you did Saturday night."

"Yeah, well, like I said, it didn't turn out exactly the way I'd planned. Maybe this Friday night will make up for it. You *are* coming, right? Your ankle okay now?"

"It will be." She wasn't staying home alone again. Not after last Saturday. Friday night, the painters would leave and they'd all go to the party at the student center, and nothing horrific would happen. A good time would be had by all.

If you really believe that, she asked herself as she hung up the phone, why are your nerves still strung as tightly as piano wire? Why do your eyes keep glancing toward the door, as if you expect someone in a weird disguise to come bursting in at any moment? Why do your ears keep listening for the sound of familiar voices out in the hall so you'll feel safe?

And why are you having such a hard time remembering what feeling safe *feels* like?

Chapter 18

That week was the worst that Maxie had spent in the house. Nerves were taut and tempers flared. The atmosphere in the house had never been worse. Two girls left, saying they were moving into dorms with friends for the time being.

Their desertions did nothing to improve the mood at Omega house. Nor did a sudden change in the weather on Friday that brought in a balmy, unexpected wave of warmth. April had arrived gently and sweetly.

But the residents of Omega house didn't believe for a minute that warm weather would improve their situation.

"Maybe," Tinker said with hope, "whoever is after us will get a sudden attack of spring fever and reform."

No one seemed to think that was likely.

"I have never been so glad to see a Friday

night arrive," Candie said as she brushed her long, auburn hair in front of Maxie's dresser mirror.

"Let's all just stick together, okay?" Maxie suggested. "I know nothing has happened to any of us *away* from the house, but that doesn't mean it couldn't."

They all agreed.

But less than an hour later, Maxie found herself sitting alone on a couch in the student center, her only companion a tall, potted plant. Brendan, after giving her a quick hug and asking about her ankle, had been dashing around ever since, seeing to party details.

Jenna had introduced her to "Skip," who really was cute, and then disappeared. Erica and Tinker had been dancing ever since they arrived, and Candie was off in a corner talking to Cath Devon, probably telling her how wise she'd been to leave Omega house.

Jenna and Skip brought her a cup of soda, kept her company for a little while, and then went off to dance again.

When Maxie realized that a whole hour had gone by, she quickly tried to locate her friends. She hadn't been keeping an eye on them after all, when she had promised herself that she would. Just in case . . .

There was no sign of any of them. She didn't

see Brendan or Erica anywhere in the huge room, Tinker wasn't on the dance floor. Graham was standing with a large group of people off to her left, but Candie wasn't with them.

A seed of worry birthed itself in Maxie's mind. So much for promising to stay together. This being one of the warmest April firsts on record, her friends might have gone outside on the terrace.

She was on her way to join them, threading her way through the dancers on the floor, when she passed Graham, dancing with a small, blonde girl.

"Where's Candie?" she asked impulsively.

He shrugged. "Candie? How would I know?"

Shaking her head, Maxie continued on her way.

The tiny seed of worry sprouted and blossomed into full-fledged concern for Candie. Where *was* everyone? If they weren't out on that terrace, Maxie was going straight to one of the security guards.

"Where are you going?" Chloe, standing at the refreshment table, called as Maxie limped by.

"To look for Candie and Erica. Come with me?"

"They're not here."

Maxie stopped just a foot shy of the glass

doors leading to the terrace. "They're not here? Where'd they go?"

"Erica lost one of her pearl earrings. The ones her grandmother gave her? We looked all over here and couldn't find it, so she said she had to retrace her steps to find it. She was really in a panic. Candie went with her to help. I offered to go, too, but Erica said one other person was enough. They should be back pretty soon."

"They went back to the house? Just the two of them?"

"Well, they've been gone a while, so I guess they didn't find the earring right outside. They must have gone back to the house." Chloe read the expression on Maxie's face and added quickly, "But there are *two* of them, Maxie. They'll be okay. It's not like Erica went all by herself. They have to come back here, anyway, because they didn't take their coats. They weren't planning on being gone that long. But," she glanced down at her watch, "maybe they decided not to come back, after all. I don't think Erica was having a very good time."

"I'm going home, too," Maxie said, deciding suddenly. "My ankle hurts and Brendan's too busy to even talk to me. If you see him, tell him I've gone, okay? Ask him to call me after the party. I'll take Erica's and Candie's coats with me, just in case they decided to stay home."

"You're not going to walk, are you? With that bad ankle?"

"It's not that far to Omega house, Chloe. But no, I guess I'll hop the shuttle. See you when you get home."

Glancing around the room in hopes of seeing Brendan or Jenna and Skip or Tinker to tell them she was leaving, and seeing no sign of any of them, Maxie picked up Erica's blue blazer and Candie's white jacket off the chair where they'd left them.

The night air had cooled considerably, and Maxie, in a long-sleeved sweater, hadn't worn a jacket. Slipping into Erica's blazer, she climbed aboard the empty shuttle.

As she took a seat in front, it occurred to her, too late, that she might miss Erica and Candie altogether. They could already be on their way back to the student center, Erica's missing earring on her ear lobe where it belonged.

Maxie felt her heart skip a beat. If they weren't there when she arrived. . . . she did *not* want to walk into an empty house. Not *that* empty house, anyway.

She would have changed her mind then, returned to the party and waited for Erica and

Candie there, or waited until someone was free to leave with her, but as she was debating, she slid one hand into a pocket of Erica's blue blazer.

Her fingers touched . . . paper. A note, maybe. None of her business. Erica's blazer, Erica's private property.

But as her fingers moved against the paper, something sharp jabbed the tip of her thumb.

Private property or not, the jab hurt. No point in Erica being stabbed, as well.

Maxie pulled the offending object free. It was wrapped loosely in the folds of a paper napkin. A napkin from the party . . . the words *April Fool* were printed on the maroon-colored paper.

Maxie unfolded the napkin to see what had stabbed her.

She recognized the earring immediately. She had seen it before, and another just like it, when the pair had been returned to Omega house after being stolen.

Erica's pearl earrings from her grand-mother.

Maxie had been stabbed by the sharp, pointy little post on the back of the earring. She turned the pearl earring over and over in her hand. Then she sat very still, the earring lying in the palm of her hand. Anyone watching the way she was staring at it might have thought she had never in her life seen anything like it.

But she was staring at it because she couldn't figure out exactly what it meant.

An earring could fall off an ear. Happened all the time. She'd lost more than one earring that way herself. An earring could even fall from one's ear into a jacket pocket without the wearer realizing it.

But . . . an earring could *not* fall off someone's ear and then promptly wrap itself up in a paper napkin.

An earring could only end up inside a wrapped paper napkin if someone *put* it there. Someone's fingers had taken that earring, wrapped it in the napkin, and put it in the blazer pocket.

Erica's blazer pocket. Erica, who had said the earring was missing. Erica, who had taken Candie with her on an earring hunt.

For an earring that wasn't missing.

Questions boiled and bubbled in Maxie's mind.

Why would someone wrap an earring in a napkin, hide it in their jacket pocket, and then tell other people the earring was missing?

Well, Maxie's inner voice suggested, didn't it make a great excuse for leaving the party? Wasn't a missing earring a great reason to return to Omega house, where there are no paint-ers standing guard outside and no house-mother, and there are no sorority sisters be-cause they're all at the party you just left? And they're going to be there for a while? So you know you'll have the house all to your-self?

Why would Erica want the house all to herself? Maxie questioned. Besides, Erica didn't *go* back to the house all alone. She took Candie with her.

Too bad for Candie, the voice answered.

Scarcely breathing, Maxie pictured tall, wide-shouldered Erica as the gray-haired, white-clothed caterer's helper she'd seen in the pantry. Then she pictured Erica as the fake Tia Maria. In her mind's eye, she slathered Erica's face with makeup, dressed her in the lime-green and hot-pink outfit, slapped a cranberry-colored wig on her head. It worked. Erica's own mother wouldn't have known her.

Then Maxie erased that picture and pictured instead Erica in a white exterminator's uni-form, a cap and sunglasses completing the pic-ture. That worked, too. Feeling as if she were playing paper dolls, Maxie then wardrobed Er-ica in a white medical coat, pushed her blonde hair up underneath a gray wig and covered half her face with a white handkerchief.

That, too, worked.

We were wrong, she thought, leaning forward to clutch at the back of the seat in front of her as nausea overtook her. We thought it was different people, maybe the friends of girls we hadn't pledged. But it *wasn't* different people. It was *one* person, in different *disguises*. Erica?

No. . . .

But she was the right size, and she had the sort of square, strong face that, without makeup and with darkened eyebrows and lashes, could pass for masculine. She had been in drama classes in high school, and would know something about makeup and disguises.

No . . . All of those people who had come to the house had been *Erica*?

Maxie struggled to think of even one instance when one of the disguised people had come to the house while Erica was there, proving that it couldn't have been her.

The catering staff? Erica had been somewhere in the house, but it wouldn't have taken that long to throw on a gray wig, a white uniform and white shoes and glasses. And she'd only been in the pantry a few minutes . . . in and out . . . just long enough to plant the garbage in the frig. Then she must have slipped up the back staircase, removed her disguise, and rejoined the group.

And, of course, she hadn't been home when the doctor showed up. The ants must have been in the black medical bag that was part of her disguise.

Where had she found so many ants?

That one was easy. Erica worked in the entomology lab two afternoons a week.

And only Chloe had been home when the fake exterminator showed up.

Maxie groaned aloud.

"You okay back there, miss?" the driver asked nervously. "Not getting sick on me, are you?"

"I'm fine," she answered, although she wasn't. Far from it.

Erica.

Omega Phi's president had been sabotaging them.

Why?

Chapter 19

The shuttle stopped at the foot of Omega's driveway. The house was dark. Maxie climbed down and stood under a streetlight, debating.

Should she wait in the driveway until the next patrol car circled the block? She could flag down the car and get help. Or would that be wasting precious moments? Candie was probably in that house alone with Erica.

Why Candie? Maxie wondered as she made her decision. She dropped the two coats on the ground and broke into an awkward, limping lope up the driveway toward the house. The heavy white scaffolding against the garage side of the house stood out against the night darkness. The painters had long since gone home. She was on her own.

Did Erica have something against Candie that no one knew about? Or was it just that Candie was *there* when Erica decided to lure one of her sisters back to the house? Would any one of the sorority sisters have suited Erica's purpose, and Candie just happened to be the unlucky one, in the wrong place at the wrong time?

What *was* Erica's purpose?

Something to do with her mother's accident? Maxie wondered as she quietly, carefully pulled the big wooden door open and stepped cautiously into the foyer. Erica's mother had been injured because of hazing for the sorority, and had limped ever since. No one had had any idea that Erica blamed Omega Phi for that. But she must. It was the only explanation that made sense.

Erica was seeking revenge for a twenty-year-old injury? That was *insane*.

The first thing Maxie noticed as she stealthily entered the house was the overpowering smell of paint. A faint glow came from the kitchen at the rear of the house and another was shining down from the upstairs hall, but the lamps that were usually left on in the living room had all been switched off.

Someone wanted the house in darkness.

At first, the only sound Maxie heard was the distant, steady *drip-drip* of the kitchen faucet. Then, as her eyes became accustomed to the near-darkness and she listened intently, scuffling sounds in the living room to her right caught her attention.

She was afraid to call Candie's name aloud. If her arrival hadn't been heard, she didn't want to announce it now. She might still have the element of surprise on her side.

Maxie tiptoed over to the wide arch leading into the living room. She stood at the entrance, peering into the darkness.

Someone was in there. She could see a figure that seemed to be dressed completely in white, moving about the room, mumbling softly as it bent and stooped, bent and stooped. Hefting something . . . Maxie peered more intently . . . large white containers. Plastic buckets with handles.

Paint containers. Huge white plastic paint containers, like the ones lined up in the garage. The figure in the living room was setting big buckets of paint all around the room, ripping the lids off them, tossing the lids aside.

The fumes made Maxie's eyes burn.

"Erica," she wanted to call out, "what are you *doing*? Stop it right now! And where is Candie? What have you done with her?"

But she knew better. The person dressed in what she now realized was a white coverall like the painters wore, a white painter's cap covering the hair and a stiff, white mask covering the lower half of the face, was so far unaware of her presence.

Best to keep it that way.

If she tried to phone for help from downstairs, she'd be overheard. But there was a phone in her room. If she could make it up there without being seen or heard, she could make a quiet call and end this awful thing right now before it was too late.

Maxie turned, lope-limped to the stairs as quietly as possible, hip-hopped up them, far more slowly than she wanted.

She had made it all the way to the top of the wide, curving staircase, breathing hard, when she misjudged the distance to the top step and fell sideways, slamming into the wooden railing and letting an involuntary "oof" escape.

The sound seemed to carry like thunder in the dark and silent house.

Maxie held her breath.

The scuffling sounds below her stopped, leaving in their place a terrifying silence.

Maxie turned her head slowly, slowly, filled with dread as she glanced fearfully down the staircase.

The figure dressed all in white, masked in white, capped in white, stood in the doorway to the living room, looking straight up at her.

Chapter 20

Keeping her eyes on the phony "painter," Maxie inched her way backward, up the final step. She had to get to the telephone in her room.

The painter began moving slowly up the stairs. "Well, hi, there, hon!" the brassy voice of the fake Tia Maria boomed. "Wasn't expecting company, sweetie, but everybody knows Omega house is well-known for its hospitality, so we'll just have to see to it that you feel right at home, okay?"

Maxie turned and ran, wincing in pain with each step as her ankle reminded her of its injury.

The footsteps on the stairs behind her failed to pick up speed. She could hear them slowly, patiently moving up the stairs with soft thuds.

Maxie felt a wave of doubt. If that was Erica in those painter's clothes, she *knew* there were telephones up here. Why wasn't she hurrying after Maxie, to stop her?

Maxie made it into her room, closed and locked the door, exhaled a huge gulp of relief, and stumbled to the telephone. Picked it up, put the receiver to her ear.

There was no dial tone.

The phone was dead.

Maxie sank to the floor, the telephone still in her hand. No wonder Erica hadn't raced up the stairs after her.

There was a light tap on the door. Then the voice of the injured "doctor," deep and confident, called, "Need any help in there? I noticed you have a bad ankle. I might be able to give you a shot for the pain." A deep, wicked chuckle. "Put you to sleep for a long time. Maybe even a *very* long time." Another laugh. "But first you'll have to open the door and let me in."

"Not in this lifetime!" Maxie shouted defiantly. She was angry, but she knew the person she was angriest with was herself. She should have waited in the driveway for the patrol car. What was the good of having the police around if you weren't willing to let them handle things?

Now, look where I am, she thought wearily. Locked in my room, no one else home, no telephone to call for help, and a maniac on the other side of the door.

She couldn't just sit here on the floor and wait for something to happen.

As she pulled herself to her feet, Maxie caught sight of the white scaffolding stationed outside her window.

No . . . I *hate* heights, she protested even as she moved to the window to look out. Heights make me dizzy and sick. I'd fall before I even got both feet on that thing.

But she opened the window and peered out. The structure stationed against the house loomed up out of the darkness like a giant Tinkertoy. The platform itself, running horizontally beneath her window, was too far down for her to step directly onto. She would have to hang from the sill and drop onto it.

Even if I could get up enough nerve to do that, she thought, dizzy just from looking out the window, I'd still have to climb down the rungs to get to the ground.

No. Impossible.

"Hey, Maxie," an unfamiliar, masculine-sounding voice called, "any bugs in there? You got creepy-crawlies I can zap with my miracle insecticide?"

The fake exterminator.

"You know, this stuff kills more than bugs,"

the voice tormented from beyond Maxie's door. "Maxie? You still in there?" A hand rattled the doorknob, lightly at first, then more violently. "Take me no more than two minutes to get this stupid door open, you hear me?" The voice was angry now, but it still didn't sound like Erica's voice. Maybe she'd used so many different voices, she'd forgotten how her own sounded.

The doorknob rattled again.

Two minutes . . .

Maxie threw one leg over the windowsill, then the other, until she was sitting on the sill. Then she turned around carefully, facing the window, placed her hands on the sill, and lowered her body toward the platform.

There were several horrible seconds when her feet touched nothing but air and she was sure she was going to completely miss the platform and fall to her death. But then the toes of her left foot touched wood, and slowly, carefully, she stretched her legs, wincing as the bad ankle protested. Stretching, stretching, her fingers aching, her arms shrieking in pain . . . her right foot touched the platform, and her hands let go of the sill.

The platform jiggled slightly as she landed, falling into a semicrouch, clutching one of the white pipelike metal supports with both hands.

The worst part was still ahead of her. She

crouched there, holding on, as long as she dared. But she knew that she had to get to the ground before her pursuer realized that she was no longer in her room.

She stood up shakily and reached out with both hands to the nearest scaffold support.

I can't *do* this, she thought with certainty as a wave of dizziness overwhelmed her.

You have no *choice*, her brain ordered. *Go! Now!*

Maxie went.

Slowly, hand over hand, down the white pole, gripping it with her legs, like a fireman sliding down a pole to a fire. She did not look down. She prayed the whole way down, and prayed harder each time she came to a place where the rungs criss-crossed each other, forming an "X" that she had to climb around before she could continue sliding.

It was a harrowing descent, made worse by the sensation of minutes ticking away rapidly. How much time did she have before Erica got the door to her room open and realized that her quarry had made its escape?

Halfway down the scaffolding, Maxie glanced toward the garage and its apartment, sitting off to the left and behind the house. Tuttle's truck was there. If she could just make it to the ground, she'd go get him, make him call for help . . .

If I can just get to the ground, Maxie prayed . . .

Her hands were wet with sweat, her legs aching from gripping the pole, her shins stinging from rubbing against the cold white metal.

Not much further . . . almost there. . . .

Tuttle might not be home. He could have gone out with friends. Did he have friends? No, he couldn't have friends, because he *had* to be home. He *had* to help her.

There . . . just below her . . . the blessed, wonderful, beautiful ground! A foot more, that was all, just twelve little inches and she'd be there. . . .

She dropped the last few inches, favoring her bad ankle so that she stood slightly tilted, leaning gratefully against the thick metal pipe of the scaffolding frame as she caught her breath.

The voice came out of the darkness, destroying every last shred of her relief at finally being back on the ground.

"Hi, there, Maxie! Nice trip down?"

The figure all in white stood before her, and although it was still wearing the stiff white mask, Maxie could feel its slow, easy, triumphant smile.

Chapter 21

"What do you *want*?" Maxie screamed, her voice shaking. "Leave me *alone*!"

"Hey, what's goin' on out there?" Tom Tuttle's voice called from the garage. Maxie heard heavy footsteps on the stairs leading down from the garage apartment.

She heaved a heartfelt sigh of relief. The gardener was coming to her rescue. Suddenly, Tuttle didn't seem quite so creepy. If he got her out of this, she would never say anything bad about the gardener again.

"Here, Tuttle!" she cried, "over here, by the side door to the utility room."

Her white-uniformed attacker darted backwards, into the shadows. But Maxie could still hear ragged breathing, coming from the bushes.

"Over there!" she shouted, pointing, as Tuttle arrived, muttering under his breath. "By those bushes."

Tuttle turned in the direction she was pointing.

The board came out of nowhere. Thick and solid, it slammed into the side of Tuttle's head, knocking him off his feet and sideways. He grunted with surprise as he flew out and then down, slamming into the ground with a fleshy-sounding thump. His head bounced once when it hit. Tuttle let out a distressed little sigh as his eyes closed and his body came to rest on the lawn.

Maxie watched the whole thing with horrified eyes, letting out a shrill scream when the board slammed into Tuttle. Then shock rendered her silent.

When the gardener was completely still, she whispered, "Why did you *do* that? I think you've . . . you've *killed* him."

"The old coot isn't dead." Tuttle's attacker emerged from the bushes. "Only the good die young." Maxie's left wrist was suddenly encircled with one of the painter's white-gloved hands, while the other hand bent to wrap itself around the gardener's overalls. Then a door was opened and both victims were dragged into the utility room, where Tuttle was deposited in a heap and Maxie was tossed into a corner, near the washing machine.

It was dark inside, the air heavy with the smell of paint. Maxie sat huddled against one wall, her arms around her knees. Her heart was pounding so loudly, she half-expected Erica to shout, "Stop that infernal noise!"

"For your information," she was told, the voice muffled behind the mask, "the door is locked. You'd never get it unlocked before I caught up with you. And I would be very, very angry that you'd tried to leave me. So forget about getting out of here. It's not going to happen."

"You can't keep me here." The defiance in her voice was forced. She was terrified. She couldn't see, but could feel, Tuttle lying so still, so crumpled up, like a pile of painters' rags.

"Guess again. I can do anything I want. And what I want is for this place to go up in smoke. So that's exactly what's going to happen. And you with it, Maximilia."

Maxie's defiance deserted her. Up in smoke? Fire?

"Let there be light," the voice that didn't sound like Erica's said, chuckling. "Can't work in the dark." There was the click of a switch, and the darkness evaporated, replaced by a garish yellow glow from an overhead bulb.

"So," the voice said, "how do you like your new accommodations? It really doesn't matter if they're not to your liking, because these are temporary lodgings. Believe me, they're *very* temporary."

Maxie's eyes went to Tom Tuttle's limp body. Although she willed him to wake up and help her, his eyes remained closed and not a muscle moved. Even if he did wake up, she knew he wouldn't be in any shape to fight.

Humming softly, the white-clothed figure picked up two of the huge white paint containers lined up against the wall and moved to the oversized white hot water heater.

Maxie watched fearfully as Erica crawled behind it.

What was happening?

Whatever it was, she was suddenly sharply aware that the tall, fat, hot water heater stood *between* her and Erica. Shielding her from view. Any move she made now couldn't possibly be seen from behind that tank. The door was on the painter's side, so Maxie couldn't very well get out, but . . .

Her heart leaped. If she approached from the left side, very quietly . . .

What she needed was a weapon of some kind, a board, a tool . . .

Her eyes searched the utility room. There

were tools. But they were on a shelving unit directly behind the painter's head. Would she have time to grab one before she was noticed?

It was worth a try.

The thought of slamming Erica on the head with a wrench or hammer made her physically ill. She wasn't at all sure she could do it. Maybe there was some other way.

What other way? The outside door was locked, the door to the house too close to her captor.

She had never hurt anyone physically in her entire life. But she had no choice now. All it would take was a light blow, enough to stun, to give her time to run into the house, unlock a door and call for help.

Before the house went up in flames fueled by paint fumes.

Stiffening her spine, Maxie took a deep breath, slid out of her loafers, and tiptoed quickly and quietly across the cement floor. She couldn't be seen, she knew that. But she also knew that at any second, that white-capped head could lift, see that she was no longer in that same spot, and Erica could jump up to grab her. With fury. At any second . . .

She was only inches from her destination. Her eyes were fixated on Erica's legs, sticking out from behind the hot water heater to make sure they didn't suddenly move. So she failed to see a painter's round green spray bottle lying on the floor. One socked foot nudged it and sent it and its green plastic tubing spinning into the wall with a loud scuttling sound.

Maxie gasped, her heart stopped, but her feet kept moving even as Erica's legs jerked in response.

Maxie rounded the hot water heater. She never took her eyes off her target for a second as she sent her arm on a search of the shelves, blindly, desperately, seeking a tool, a shovel, a weapon of some kind. Anything . . .

She wasn't close enough. Her fingers curled around nothing but air.

Erica, alerted by the noise the paint sprayer had made, stood up.

Turned around.

Saw her.

Brown eyes blazed with fury. "I *knew* I should have creamed you the way I did Tuttle, you witch! I figured, since you couldn't get *out* of here, I'd let you watch what I was doing. Gave me a kick, having you watch. My mistake . . ."

There was no time for Maxie to turn and run. There was only enough time to realize, with a paralyzing sense of shock, that the eyes blazing anger and hatred at her were *brown*.

The figure lunged at her, forcing her up against the wall, hands at her throat.

Erica's eyes were *blue*.

The figure pushed her closer to the shelves.

Oh, Erica, Maxie thought, I'm sorry. I'm really sorry. I should have known it wasn't you.

Choking, gagging, she sent her hand on another search. This time, her fingers closed around something metal, something hard . . . lifted it . . . sent it down upon the white-capped skull . . .

But at the last minute, her attacker saw it coming and moved, receiving only a glancing blow to the temple. It was enough to force her cruel hands away from Maxie's throat, but not enough to knock out the attacker.

Shattered by the lost opportunity, knowing she wouldn't get another chance, Maxie thought grimly, *Okay, then*, and reached out with her free hand to rip the stiff white painter's mask free.

And gasped in disbelief.

Chapter 22

"*Candie?*" Maxie was so stunned, she offered no resistance when Candie reached out and shoved her to the floor. She sat with her back against the wall, looking up, her eyes wide with disbelief. "But . . . I thought you were Erica," Maxie whispered.

"Well I'm not, am I? I'm Allison Barre's baby daughter, Candace. The one she never had time for." Candie's voice was laced with bitterness.

"It was you all the time? You were the woman in the caterer's uniform? You were the doctor, the exterminator, Tia Maria?"

Candie, the white cap still covering her auburn waves, leaned against the hot water heater. "My, you've got a mind like a steel trap. Not that it's going to do you any good, being so smart." She folded her white-shirted arms over her chest and smiled down at Maxie.

"Still, you *are* going to go out in a blaze of glory. You interrupted me just now, but when I've finished what I started, you and this horrible old house are going to go up in flames like Fourth of July fireworks."

"This horrible old house?" Maxie stared up at her. "I thought you loved this place. You said you did."

Candie shrugged. "So I lied. Sue me." Then rage filled her face and she bared her teeth. "I *hate* this place! I always have. I only came here to do what I promised myself I'd do when I was ten years old and *she* drove my father away. A year later, my brother couldn't take it anymore, and he left, too. They left me there alone. With *her*."

Maxie's ankle throbbed and in an unconscious effort to relieve the pain, she changed its position. As she did so, it bumped gently up against the paint sprayer she had accidentally kicked earlier. "Her? Your mother?"

Candie sneered. "Some *mother* she was. Allison Barre, the toast of Omega Phi Delta, secretary, then vice president, and then, at long last, president. She never got over it. Never stopped talking about it, never stopped wanting it back, never loved *anything* as much as she did those four years. Not my father, not my brother, not me. Especially not me."

The plastic paint sprayer had a fat, clear hose attached to its nozzle. Maxie followed the hose with her eyes as she listened to Candie. The hose trailed across the floor of the utility room and stretched its way to one of the squat, fat white plastic containers of paint.

Candie turned and began marching back and forth beside the hot water heater, swinging her arms as she walked. "We could have had such a great family. My father adored her. He couldn't believe he'd won the prize of Salem University. They were married right after her graduation. She wanted to stay here, settle down in Twin Falls, didn't want to leave the university. But my father had a job in Philadelphia, so they had to go. He told me when he left us that she'd never forgiven him for taking her away from here. He was right. She never had."

Maxie lifted her left leg, hooked her foot over the spray bottle and slid it back toward her, hoping Candie wouldn't notice, praying it wouldn't scrape against the floor tiles. It didn't. When it was close enough and Candie's back was turned momentarily, she reached out, grabbed the bottle and hid it behind her.

How did the spray bottle work?

"She was still in the sorority, of course," Candie raved on, stomping back and forth, back and forth, swinging her arms. "It's for *life*, remember? She told you all that the day of the tea. She'd been telling *me* that every single day of my life. 'Once a sister, always a sister,' and nobody believed that more than she did. I don't think she ever thought of anything else."

Maxie kept one hand behind her, her fingers exploring the sprayer, searching for the right knob or lever that would suck the paint up into the hose and send it on its way, out through the round nozzle. But she kept her eyes on Candie every second.

"She was never home. And when she was, she was on the phone — with one of her 'sisters.' She never even came to any of my plays in high school, she was so busy with her stupid sorority activities. And the whole time, the whole time I was growing up, she made it so clear," there were tears in Candie's angry voice now, "that she would have done anything, *anything*, including trading in her family, to be back here at Omega house, reliving those four glorious years."

There, a small round knob . . . Maxie turned it slowly, carefully, and watched with a pounding pulse as the clear hose began to fill with thick white paint. The spray bottle would fill quickly.

Candie whirled to face Maxie, her cheeks red with rage. For one terrible second, Maxie was certain Candie would notice the clear plastic hose turning white with goo.

But Candie was too caught up in her rage to notice anything. "She didn't *want* to be with us!" she cried. "She wanted to be back *here*! In this house . . . this horrible, terrible house that I hate more than anything!"

"It isn't Omega Phi's fault, or the fault of anyone in the house now," Maxie said. After a moment, she added, "You stole your own ring, didn't you? And sent it back by messenger. After you'd taken Erica's jewelry box. Why did you send them back?"

"Oh, that was just the beginning," Candie said smugly. "Just a message. To let everyone in the house know that something was going on. That's all that was."

"You wanted us to think it was Graham," Maxie realized. "I almost did. But when I asked him tonight at the party where you were, he said 'How should I know?' That's not what you'd say if you were fixated on someone, is it? I didn't get it then, but he *wasn't* calling you and sending you flowers and writing you notes, was he, Candie? You made all of that up. He just sees you as a friend, that's all. And you

198

deliberately started that argument with him on campus that day because you knew I'd be along any minute, to meet you for lunch. You knew I'd think he was bothering you."

Candie just smiled smugly and nodded. Maxie went on, "You sprayed insecticide on the plates, didn't you? That's how you knew what happened and let it slip when you were pretending to be Tia Maria. Did you tell me on purpose, or was it an accident?"

"Careless of me," Candie said, beginning to stride back and forth again. "I forgot that I'd already told you guys my mother didn't know anything about what was going on."

"But . . . but you got sick, too, that night." Maxie wrapped her fingers tightly around the jar, still hidden behind her. If she didn't have her thumb on the right knob . . .

"Oh, I most certainly did not! I told you, my mother missed some great performances when she skipped my plays. I'm quite an accomplished actress, Maxie. I wasn't sick at all. I'm not stupid enough to spray my own plate with insecticide. Anyway," Candie added casually, "it was Mildred's fault. I was planning on spraying the pot of spaghetti, in which case the police would have found the insecticide. I hadn't thought of that. But when I saw all the plates, so neatly set around the table, and knew they'd be washed after dinner, well, it just made sense to use them instead. Mildred shouldn't have set the table so early."

"We could have been killed." Maxie gripped the jar more tightly, slid it just a fraction of an inch to the right, toward the outside edge of her skirt.

"Oh, I only sprayed a tiny bit on each plate. I didn't want you all dead. Not then. I was saving that for tonight."

"What are you going to do, Candie? Why were you fiddling with the hot water heater? And why all the paint cans in the living room?" As if she didn't know the answer. But keeping Candie talking seemed like the best idea right now.

But her question had exactly the opposite effect. "Enough talk," Candie said curtly, and dropped to her knees beside the hot water tank again, her back to Candie. "I told you, this house I've hated all of my life is going to go up in a blaze of glory, and you're going with it."

"That won't change anything, Candie. It won't make your mom change."

Candie's head swivelled in fury. "Yes, it *will*! No house, no sorority. No sorority, no fixation, period. She'll get over it. And she'll come to *me* for comfort when it's all gone."

"Omega Phi is more than a house, Candie. You know that's true. What your mom wants back is in her *head*, in her memory, not in this house. She'll just hate you for what you've done, that's all."

"She'll never know. No one will. Because you're not going to be around to tell them. And no one else knows. I *was* planning on blowing *all* of you to kingdom come tonight after everyone was asleep. But that didn't work out. I guess it'll just have to be you and Erica."

"Where *is* Erica?"

Candie pointed. "Over there. In that closet. Folded up like dirty laundry." She laughed. "She never even knew the earring fell off . . . I scooped it up and wrapped it in a napkin and stuck it in her blazer pocket. I knew she'd freak when she noticed it was missing. She'd want to retrace her steps. It was the perfect way to get her back here. I'm going straight back to the dance when I finish with the house."

"Chloe knows you left with Erica."

"Chloe's an idiot. I'll just say Erica went home alone and I returned to the dance. Everyone will think what you thought. That she was angry about her mother's accident and wanted revenge. You *did* think that, right, Maxie?"

Maxie flushed with pain. I'm sorry, Erica, she thought again.

Suddenly, Candie smiled at Maxie, a brilliant, happy smile. "I saw this on television," she said cheerfully, bending again to the hot water heater. "You just unhook this little whatchamacallit back here, set the paint cans around, open the lids, and the paint fumes mixed with the leaking gas ignite. Fireworks! And Omega house, the only place my mother was ever really happy, will be history. And so will nosy Maximilia McKeon. But first, I have to tie you up. . . ."

As Candie stood up and sent her eyes on a search around the room, Maxie slid the spray canister out from behind her and checked quickly to make sure it was loaded.

It was.

She jumped to her feet, her thumb on what she prayed was the correct knob, and yelled Candie's name to make her turn around.

"What?" Candie said impatiently, and turned.

Maxie aimed the jar at Candie's face and jabbed the knob with her thumb.

It was the correct knob.

A spray of white paint flowed forth instantly, right in Candie's face. Candie screamed out in horror, and her hands flew to her eyes.

Maxie took advantage of her surprise attack.

Running to the door leading into the kitchen, she pulled it open and ducked inside.

And at that moment, Maxie heard the sound of a car door slamming outside.

Her sisters were home.

Chapter 23

Two hours later, surrounded by friends gathered in her room, Maxie commanded, "Will you all please stop looking at me like I was Joan of Arc? It makes me nervous."

"Well, you *did* save the house . . . and everyone who lives here," Tinker said. "You said yourself, Candie had planned to do her dirty work when we were all in bed. If you hadn't showed up when you did and stopped her, she wouldn't have had to change her plans. Nothing would have happened until we were all in bed and asleep." She shuddered. "Everything . . . everything would be gone, and us with it."

Brendan and Jenna, summoned to the house by a grateful Erica, nodded agreement. "It was crazy of you to tackle Candie alone," Brendan scolded gently. But he took her hand in his as he said it.

"I guess," Jenna admitted reluctantly, "life in a sorority house isn't as dull as I thought it was, is it?"

That brought a sad, rueful laugh from everyone in the room. They all knew it would be a long time before everything seemed the same as it had once been. Maybe that would never happen.

"Look," Maxie felt compelled to point out, "I should have figured all of this out sooner. The thing was, I knew I'd noticed something important when Tia Maria was doing my so-called makeover. I just couldn't remember what it was. Now, I do."

Erica, nursing a headache from the blow to her skull delivered by Candie, spoke up from her place on Tinker's bed. "What was it, Maxie?"

"She was wearing Candie's ring. I mean, she had all these rings on her fingers, over her plastic gloves, like she couldn't bear not to have them on. One of them looked so familiar . . ." Maxie grimaced. "Could have saved us all a lot of heartache, if I'd realized that earlier."

Brendan laughed. "Will you just relax and let yourself be patted on the back a little? We," waving his hand to include the entire group, "believe in giving credit where credit is due. Enjoy. It won't last that long."

Maxie squeezed Brendan's hand. Then she looked around at Jenna and all her sisters and smiled.

At last, they were all safe.

Last Date

Call me.

Oh yes. Yes. She was used to telling people what to do. Used to getting what she wanted.

Used to having it all.

Call me.

To her, it was just a game. Her game. Her rules.

But the rules had just changed. And she was about to find out.

It wasn't a game anymore. Not a dating game.

Now it was the dying game.

Could she play by the rules of the dying game?

No.

Probably not.

But she'd have a chance. A chance to prove herself worthy.

Pity death always won in the end. . . .

About the Author

"Writing tales of horror makes it hard to convince people that I'm a nice, gentle person," says **Diane Hoh**.

"So what's a nice woman like me doing scaring people?

"Discovering the fearful side of life: what makes the heart pound, the adrenalin flow, the breath catch in the throat. And hoping always that the reader is having a frightfully good time, too."

Diane Hoh grew up in Warren, Pennsylvania. Since then, she has lived in New York, Colorado, and North Carolina, before settling in Austin, Texas. "Reading and writing take up most of my life," says Hoh, "along with family, music, and gardening." Her other horror novels include *Funhouse*, *The Accident*, *The Invitation*, *The Fever*, and *The Train*.

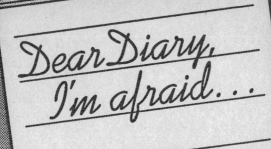

Dear Diary,
I'm afraid...